SWI
SEN

Claudia Bellocq

Equinox 2013
To Liz & Erin
love & lust!
Steph aka Claudia
xxx

ONEIROS BOOKS

In association with
WWW.PARAPHILIAMAGAZINE.COM

First published in the world by ONEIROS 2012

Copyright Claudia Bellocq

Claudia Bellocq asserts the amoral right to be
identified as the author
of this work.

ISBN 978-1-291-16528-9

Born in 2007-2008, or rather hatched, these collected works let you into the darkest corners of my imagination, experiences, thoughts and feelings.

It's a place where thoughts freefall into burning fires; feelings run amok alongside chaos dancers of the wildest, most untamed nature. Punctuation is cast aside in favour of the spewing of language onto the page, the translation of thought into form...

Enjoy them, inject them, inhale them, fuck them, dance with them, hold them, weep with them, do whatever you please with them as long as they captivate you for a moment or two...

Love and bullets,

Redlight Razorgirl a.k.a Claudia Bellocq

~ Dedicated to ~

My Children and My Liberation,

And to all the wild, untamed spirits of the world.

witch.

baba yaga the witch sat picking at the bones of the men she had eaten that night. tearing. pulling at the remaining flesh, snapping the fragile parts and tossing them aside with a violent gesture of her bony, knotted hands.

"hissssssssssssssssssssss, hisssssssssssssssssssss, hisssssssssssssssss," she spat. laughing aloud; practicing scaring the ones she planned to eat tonight. they cowered in a corner of her dingy cave and wept for their lovers, their wives and their children.

"oh hush now my pretty's...it's really all very, *very* sweet. you're going to relish being eaten by me almost as much as i'm going to relish eating you," as she opened her yellow old mouth, curled her lip and clashed her metal teeth - newly sharpened.

one of the men, on seeing the bones she was foraging over, let out a whimper.

"you, you with the pretty little cry, come over here....."

the man begged. the witch hiked up her dress. black and dusty as old crows feathers, violent purple undertones, scarred skinny legs and the mother of a gash between her thighs, she showed him her cunt. it was snapping its metal teeth...

her black, laced-up boots distracted him a moment. thankful...

"shall i fuck you or eat you?" she was toying with him.

"well pretty boy, what's it to be?"

he whimpered again and began begging for a stay of the inevitable execution. silently or aloud, he wasn't sure which. no-one could hear him though so it must've been a silent prayer.

baba yaga's bite was opium filled sweetness. on first contact it imparted a considerable amount of some heavy, delirium inducing substance that sent her victims all trance and willing. they would smile at her, an idiotic fool's smile, and approach her, complicit in their own deaths. desperate to know what secrets she held. desperate to offer themselves to her. she had a challenge on her door you see...scratched into the splintered wood, you could just about read (faded now from years of existence):

'if any one of you sorry souls can please me, you will stand beside me in all eternity. death or eternity? in your hands.'

of course this made them all want to try for eternity and the witch got at least a good fuck before she ate them. try or die...no contest.

the one who was whimpering glanced uneasily around her cave. damp walls seeping some kind of ever present slimy fluid. the sound of water drip, drip, dripping in the distance, magnified by echo. a corner, sacred it would seem, full of tiny blue, brown, black, violet bottles all stopped up with fur, grasses and bits of wood. in the middle, a very. clearly. marked. out. altar of sorts and in the middle of *that*, a birds skull, a snakeskin and an eagles wing surrounded by what looked like unintelligible gibberish texts. crooked birds feet hanging from the low ceiling, along with the pelts of many a dead animal and god knows what else. candles spilling their waxy cum all over the floor, some still burning, others long since satiated.

"you, you who would gaze upon me in so much fear, come closer..."

he approached.

her breath; her breath stank of acrid tobacco and stale men. around her a smell of sex, burning sage and sweetgrass. the sacred and the profane all mixed up together. it was fucking with his ability to discern if this witch was his creator or destroyer. he could see her teeth, her mouth and her cunt all mixed up now, snapping, hungry, biting, bitching.

she bit him and he felt himself starting to fall into a vortex of pleasurable pain, not sure where he was any more, or why he was here, or how he got there....

floating, fucking, eating, being eaten, devouring, savouring, feasting, swimming into pools of ecstatic tides of deep indigo seas that belonged to another time, another place. a place before birth. back there he surrendered. a sea of souls surrounded him, exquisite, unspoiled. pure. pure ecstasy. and he remembered this place. just as she did every time she fucked/ate her men.

baba yaga. hungry. the sea of souls calling. a siren. a cursing, demented, lamenting song. a cry to liberty.

witch.

doll

dead eyes barbie doll lolling over to the left of you. vacant stare as her little plastic cunt yearns for kens cock. once she dreamed of skin, of flesh, of eyes that moved and saw things. then she remembered she was plastic. dead eyes barbie doll.

ripple muscle ken watches dead eyes barbie and imagines fucking her hard up her pink plastic cunt. hey doll...how you doin' baby....then he remembers he has no cock, only a space where it should have been and he weeps and curses mattel™ as hard as a silent plastic man doll can.

barbie is a slut he says. whatever. never wanted her anyway. gets his camouflage on and gets down with the boys in all manner of action poses. home.

barbie is getting cocky now. watching ken with the boys. jesus what a dork, how could i even have thought about it she gasps, heady, breathless, coquettish and still plastic. turns to the girls and goes shoe shopping and dressing up in pink frills and feather trim. home.

barbie knows ken could hurt her
ken knows barbie could kill him.

barbie is becoming animated. her plastic is getting a life of its own these days. she likes how it feels and doesn't want to go back to plastic a-go-go land.

ken is waking up and wonders if sleep was more comfortable. feel. feel. feel. where's my grenades he wonders realising there's a dick starting to grow where the plastic space was.

barbies panties are no longer the flat white asexual cover they once were. barbie tries to hide her cunt.

ken has seen it. plastic to plastic becoming heart to heart.

barbie wants to run and ken shouts "fuck off then...go!"

ken wants to back off and barbie shouts "yeah right, been there done that, dick face."

"dick face? wow! i've got a dick," preens ken proudly.

barbie loves ken

ken loves barbie

they become human and squeeze themselves uncomfortably into their new form

hoping.

doll ii

barbie: "ken, you know you want me baby"
ken: "whatever barb"
football results on in background. barbie pacing. plastic heels killing her. plastic toes permanently on end. plastic cunt permanently dry.
barbie: "baby....i'm melting here. hungry for you honey. come to bed ken."
ken: "yeah sweetness...soon" - back to football.
disco music on in background. bedroom pink; too pink. thinks 'jesus, gimme a bratz anyday, no edge to this bitch, but i guess one plastic cunt is as good as another.'
ken: "yeah baby, keep it hot for me honey, on my way."
their first time. should be fucking amazing. should be all blow out and punctures. should deflate plastic. leaves them cold. ken's cock shrinking when he's only just got it. barbie's cunt fading to grey/white space again.
barbie: "ken honey, you wanna make a baby?"
ken: silence
barbie: "ken honey, you wanna make a baby honey? you hear me? saw a new version of myself last week. detachable belly. brand new home. nappies. buggy. breast feeding chair. bottle for baby. sopping wet nipple pads. bloody sanitary towels. screaming insanity. no sleep."
ken looking at brand new barbie model without detachable belly.
ken and barbie get it on

fuck fuck fuck. oooh baby. ooh doll. no cum. no cum
shit, forgot you couldn't cum. no baby.
barbie leaves ken
ken weeps.
bratz....

excavated

we were walking beside the canal, you and me. kicking the odd stone into the river, poking at the odd dog turd with a stick, flicking each other with the sharp ends of old bits of flotsam we found drifting along in the current. it was sunny.

you stopped and turned to me and said "you read about that girl they excavated last week. down that pit not far from here?"

"no" i said "where's that then?"

"the old tin mine round the end of the canal; wanna go?"

and that's when our lives changed. from stick tricks to death licks in one moment. one tiny decision. one second of no hesitation. adventure weren't it....

you looked me in the eye "you serious" you said. "you really wanna go," and i said "yeah, why not...nothing else to do"

so we walked down the canal different already. we started young, innocent kind of, on that walk. sticks and turds and playful prods. by the time we left at dusk we were all grown up. dark, cynical and changed beyond measure. i liked you both ways though but i couldn't understand you dark. for a while, i thought i'd lost you. before that, i would go "hey, alfie, you remember that time when we chased those boys and got to them, all breathlesss and sweet and didn't know what to say, so we just stared at them and left?" and you heard "blah blah blah blah blah blah blah" least it seemed that way. then you said "hey rosie, i fuckin' love you you know" and i heard "you're really sweet" and i didn't want to be sweet any more. that's why i said yes when you asked me to go to the mine. to the excavation.

we walked slower after we'd agreed to go. kind of subconsciously delaying the moment of change, when our lives would never be the same. i knew it, so did you. slow walk. dawdle like our mothers hated: like it pissed them off so bad we'd do it more.

the mine.

alfie and rosie arrive at the mine. it's late afternoon. hot sunny and there are midges everywhere. the smell of sun on skin is arousing them. there are cordoned off areas "police. scene of investigation. no entry" but there's no-one around. yesterday's news, well a bit more than yesterday but the tape is still there. alfie says "rosie, see there" and points "that's where it was" and rosie says "oh."

alfie looks at rosie and they approach the 'scene of the crime.' tentative. looking at their own shadows crossing the 'scene.' "your shadow is massive" says rosie, not knowing what else to say. ridiculous. 'god he'll think i'm so stupid.' blush.

"stand next to me rosie." it's weird here. intense. brooding.

alfie imagines the girl, then leans to rosie, friends since nursery, and kisses her.

rosie looks suprised. rosie *is* suprised. rosie liked it though and so her hot little lips respond to her hot little friend. before you know it rosie and alfie are pulling at each other's clothes and falling to their knees. what is it about teenage sex that makes them all fall to their knees. no finesse. no style. grabbing. grabbing tits. fingers inside panties. pushing. begging. breathing heavy. alfie still imagining the girl they found. rosie oblivious, except to the sun on her skin. and alfie inside her now.

they fucked hard and rosie thinks she 'came.' alfie knows he did. they button up their clothes and leave the mine. they hear the girls cries on their backs but they keep walking. changed.

excavated.

faint

the gasp from the audience was audible. the woman had fainted, right there in front of everyone, and as she fell her dress has somehow ended up all twisted and caught up in her legs, revealing her panties. who was going to go and mess with that?! could anyone help her without being perceived as perverted. you see, her panties were crotch-less, you know the kind…like the ones you buy in cheap sex shops, made of the worst quality nylon that becomes static at the first touch. still, if you were rubbing pussy through those, perhaps, as there was no crotch in them, the static wouldn't be an issue? anyway, i digress….

the woman's cunt was on full display. she had fallen in such a way that there was no elegance or dignity in her pose. in fact, she looked rather like a plastic blow up doll, all open-legged, pouty-mouthed and ever-ready and this made her friends, colleagues and the audience extremely uncomfortable. someone really needed to move, to do something with her, for her, but time had frozen for a split second and everyone's fantasies had come spilling out.

"oh my god, look what she's wearing"

"jesus darling, avert your eyes would you"

"god you look like a dog with your tongue hanging out like that"

"i'd fuck her and let you watch baby"

"those tights are so cheap, do you think she's a whore?"

"fucking bitch needs a good hard cock in there"

"oh, i'm really hot now. i hope i'm not blushing, it must be so obvious...do you think anyone will be able to tell that i'm turned on by a woman?"

"would you like it if i wore panties like those colin?"

etcetera, etcetera, etcetera.

why wasn't she stirring yet? as everyone twitched away, praying for someone else to do something or for something else to happen, a man in the audience started slow clapping. everyone turned to stare at him and so he stood up. dressed in a sharp black suit, well-cut, expensive, good aftershave, silk shirt, casually open button at the top of his shirt revealing just a hint of a clearly well-toned, hairy chest. sexy; he was indisputably sexy. dark hair discretely gelled into place but wouldn't you just love to run your hands through that? deep brown eyes that looked as if they could see through all of the fantasies still hanging in the air. a level stare ahead as he continued clapping. someone coughed; uncomfortable.

"darling, is it really appropriate for that man to clap? i think it's in very poor taste..."

her husband stood up and joined in with the clapping.

"oh darling do sit down....what – "

"shut up would you dear"...and he carried on clapping.

then another, and another and another until the auditorium was full of the sound of applause.

the woman who had fainted stirred a little, pushed some hair back from her eyes and looked down at herself. she straightened her dress, stood up slowly and took a bow. to the left, the centre and the right, she bowed. she looked to the man who had started the clapping and smiled a familiar, slow, sexual smile. no-one need have been there at that moment.

voyeurs, all of them.

the audience left the building, confused. left with their fantasies, the awkward, the violent, the yearning, the ineffectual, the pathetic, the sorry, the lustful, the lame, the passionate, the revealing, the damn hot and fucking horny…all of them filing out of the theatre now.

"sweetheart, was that part of the play?"

confused.

and the woman, she slipped backstage, changed her crotchless panties for lace and seamed nylons and went to meet her lover, who was waiting for her, all black suit, well cut and expensive, at the stage door. he smiled at her;

"god marlene, you're an evil bitch sometimes. i don't know how long you'll carry on getting away with that shit…"

then they left together, his hand on her ass as they walked away from all of that mess.

leaving

curled up tighter than a walnut shell, she felt her belly in knots and closed herself even further down. a silent "gggaaaaaaahhhhh" escaped her throat and took flight; black, crooked, one-winged and charred. hell visible in every direction, she glanced up to grasp the remains of the light which were slowly disappearing over the headland. leaving. i'm leaving. flight; i dream of it...it haunts me. i have to find the bastard who came in here when i was sleeping and stole my wing. ripped it from me, harsh, uncaring, brutal and left in its place a lacerated wound, dripping, raw and open and it took a fucking age to heal. i have something for him...

she fingered the pistol in the pocket on her thigh.

leaving. i'm leaving again. hard. tough shell. knotted and spitting venomous thoughts she hissed at anyone who came close to her.

'warning! this bitch bites' someone had painted in crude red letters outside her window. broken glass, empty bottles, tossed aside. bones and bits of old feathers coated in droppings now from the creatures who lived on the higher ledges.

every time she came nearer to taking flight again, she had to go through this process. remembering her stolen wing. remembering the ease of her flight before the rupture. faint now. taking herself on some masochistic journey of longing and fear....all mixed up now and making no sense. desire, yearning, sickening. loss.

poised on the ledge, she looked around her as night fell. black already the sky; better than the unforgiving daylight. she snarled as some automaton flew too close. curled her lip and gestured rudely at him/her/it/whatever the fuck it was. "fuck you" she yelled from the bottom of her lungs. coughing up bile with the force of her rage. jesus these creatures were simple. flying for the pleasure of it, never wondering what it was like to fly with one damaged wing or to fly outside the city boundaries. "fuck them all" she said, quietly this time…"fuck them all".

pain. she prepared to meet it again. drank her fill from the weird liquid she had discovered by accident one day when scouring her window-ledges for leftover food. it dulled the pain….flying was like this now; an ordeal. but what a buzz. knowing she was going beyond the city limits. knowing she had a purpose now. she preened her skin-feathers and licked harder and harder as she began to focus on her goal.

freedom

art

the mirror shattered, almost precisely at the moment of her orgasm. she took it as a sign of things to come; she was like that. her flame red hair made an exquisite fan over the crumpled pillow. she was aware of the shapes she made; her passion, her body, all curves and delight. her lover was aware of it too (though not engaged with the beauty of the pattern made by the shape of her hair on the pillow at this precise post-coital moment in time).

she wanted a photograph. aesthetics pleased her.

"baby....take a picture for me would you...there's a love...."

hun, i'm watching the match. can it wait?"

"but ba-a-by (plaintive now)...you know how these moments get lost. it's beautiful and i want it now."

"fuck's sake stella, can't you just wait? why d'you need a fucking photo every time anyway? why can't you just fuck, cum and chill like other girls do?"

stella lay still as stone. ice replacing fire now. something akin to rage bubbling (not very far) below the surface.

"am i an artist baby? is that how you see me? is that what you love about me?"

"you know it baby"

"then come and take my fucking picture before i go and find someone else to take it! .....sweetie....."

dangerous sugar in her voice.

it's true that she was an aesthete of every sense. visual images would make her cry. aural attacks would either entrance or horrify her. touch would undo her. smells both attracted and repelled her in equal measure, and she was as much entranced by those that repelled her as she by those that pleasured her in a more obvious way. the smell of her worn panties as erotically charged as the pink centre of a lily. the stink of a new york sewer as intriguing as the fragrant skin of a baby.

stella made art, with a capital a. she gave herself over to her art so much that it pained her. art was her self harm...her cutting of flesh. when she created a new piece, afterwards she would lie spent; everything threatened. she could not love when she was making new pieces. she couldn't communicate outside of her own little world...perhaps that's why her lover didn't want to take a photograph right now? knew she would be gone quick as a flash if an idea took hold, and then the battle would commence as usual.

he was tired, but he could no more conceive of loving any other woman than he could conceive of refusing stella her whims and desires. that's just how it was, for both of them.

stella looked over at him, her beloved. he was watching the match with headphones on now, momentarily safe from her demands. she loved him deeply....his idiosyncratic little ways, his total submission to his own art; music. she watched him like a voyeur watching a girl in a public toilet when he was immersed in his world. vinyl on steel. whip across skin. needle on plastic, teeth into flesh. a bass beat, a fist. a harmony, suspension held in the moment before orgasm.

when he played, he would rock his torso in a repetitive motion of endless appreciation of a rhythm, a tune...he would drag hard on his cigarette and inhale the lyrical beauty of the song he was involved with and the nicotine entering his lungs. beauty....art with a capital a.

sometimes they would fight. she wanted her art now; he was taking a breather. he would discover a riff and call her up, excited about something or other, the riff beating out in the background.

"stella…you gottta come round baby….i need you!"

"i'm in the middle of a piece babe…no can do…sorry"

click. dial tone….she was gone as simple as that. emptiness.

masturbatory sex. masturbatory art.

he loved her. she loved him.

art.

virtue

the brilliant white light of virtue was hurting her eyes. she had to look away. she found the whiteness ugly.

at this precise moment, she was standing in a cornfield beside her friend, next to the beautifully varnished oak door frame of the newly built, brand spanking new, 'peace and divinity centre.'

"did you know they were doing this?" she asked her friend.

"well yeah, only not how it would turn out of course."

"it disturbs me" she said…"something about it disturbs me, but i can't quite put my finger on it."

the party was in full swing. deva premal on the stereo, the smell of incense burning on the breeze, more people in long white clothes than she'd seen in one space for quite some time. the hospital was probably the last time, she thought to herself and laughed inside at her bitchiness.

someone passed her with a bottle of handmade elderflower cordial atop an elegant silver tray. the label was all pretty laura ashley style flowers, surrounding a penman's hand written note: 'flowers collected from the beautiful wye valley, spring 2006.' she could just see them all now, out there in their peruvian cotton clothes, all children in need but no needy children, plucking blossoms off well-loved trees.

"you got any j.d. to go in that?" she asked the woman carrying the tray. the woman didn't answer her, but looked at her, puzzled, then continued with her tray. she walked s.l.o.w.l.y and deliberately, each step enunciated like a children's bbc story reader would utter their words.

"fucking hippies" she snarled under her breath.

everyone was so calm…so fucking virtuous. it seemed to her that any one of them could just take off at any moment, levitate to a higher plane and then hover above crying out, "oh darling…it's so beautiful up here…you really must come and join me," and float some more. a woman approached them…

"so, how do you two know jen and keith?" she asked.

"oh, you know…fucked keith before he got rid of his dick and jen's an old mate," she imagined herself saying. what actually came out was:

"oh, well, we've known them both for years, haven't we suze?" but her friend was gone.

"…went to school with jen but she wasn't so weird back then" she said.

the woman adopted a patronising tone:

"so you equate peace with weird do you?"

"fuck no! just this kind of peace…i mean look at it all will you. there's not one man in this fucking party could stand up to me if i called him out. if i mentioned sex, it would be all tantra and breath and no dirt and sweat. if i mention love it would be all virtue and adoration but no passion and fighting. there would be no doubt….only servitude. if i mention uncertainty, i would probably find it packaged up on the mantelpiece along with a donations box for group healing or assistance. ya know…it just bothers me that there are no shadows here. i don't get with that. that's not peace, that's just war waiting to happen."

she turned to the woman beside her, who looked at her blankly, then gave a faint smile before turning and leaving.

suze came back with a large glass of red wine for each of them.

"best i could do" she said.

"don't fucking leave me again right! this place is full of fucking smiling stepford wives and their adoring spouses. jesus…give me a real cock now please would you suze."

"you're so angry sometimes stell….don't you fancy a bit of kuntalini without the kunt then?"

they both spat out their wine with laughter.

"shit man, let's go dancing babe"

"kay…."

the light was still shining as they made their way into the city.

twilight beckoned.

drowning

the girl woke from her dream bathed in sweat. her tangled sheets effectively binding her legs, she flailed around in panic, thrashing her arms, still trying to stop herself from drowning in the old victorian pool in which she'd been swimming just before she lost control and began to sink.

there was an eddy of water in the centre of the pool, deep, blue, crystal, inviting. curious as ever, she had swum toward it fascinated by its shapes and colour, the divine allure of the mystery, the unknown. as she flicked her toe towards the heart of the pool, she noticed a circle of people inside it. how the fuck does that work? i'm in a fucking swimming pool and there's a bunch of people in the water, on the bottom of the pool?

she knew she was dreaming.

closer to them now, she swam in circles, quietly, as still as possible, now was not the moment for flashy front crawl or butterfly stroke. "look mummy, i can do floating without moving my arms!" gentle movements of her legs keeping her afloat; she'd have to dive to get a handle on this one.

she became creature. still human but more like ariel the mermaid with scales, and a big, beating underwater heart. fuck! they were smoking crack down there! as she neared the strange group, she could see that they were smoking crack and that *she* was one of them! she watched herself…..pipe coming round now.

someone had washed the rocks (easy in a pool, though the chemicals were seeping into the water making her feel a bit queasy actually) and was now passing the pipe. men, all men besides her. she looked at them, each hovering over the pipe like a falcon with a hunt, all wings covering prey...it's mine...fuck off...it's mine.

the pipe came next to her now. she could feel the thrill of the bitter rock smoke before it hit her throat. her brain was taking the hit and becoming orgasmic before she even toked on the thing. then something happened; the man passed it over her head or was it through her, to the man on the other side of her, bypassing her as if she wasn't there.

rage erupted.

"you fucking misogynistic bastard!" she screamed at him..."you fucking arsehole" "you fucking total fucking wanker!" hysterical now the pool was starting to become all churned up and the men were getting twitchy.

"sit down bitch! you're stirring up the water. you wanna get us all killed?"

beyond stopping.

"that pipe...it was my turn...why d'you fucking pass me over like that dick-brain?"

the water twisted like an ugly dancer. all caught up in it now only the others had vanished and the girl was alone in the core of the whirlpool, where it felt pleasantly empty for a while, spacious even. then the first black water entered her lungs. she choked, coughed, panicked a little. filling her lungs fast now she began to thrash her legs hard to get to the surface of the pool, the water sucking her deeper the more she thrashed. losing any sense of balance or alignment, the top could have been the bottom for all she knew.

at this point of surrender, she blacked out and sank slowly into the darkness. comfortable, deep inky blue-black darkness.

"someone pass me that fucking pipe now would you...stop fucking about"....calm.....

she hit it at the precise moment of her orgasm.

she woke with the sheets all tangled round her legs, dripping in sweat, palms sticky, cunt wet, panic in her throat.

a natural disaster is the consequence of the combination of a natural hazard (a physical event e.g. volcanic eruption, earthquake, landslide) and human activities. human vulnerability, caused by the lack of appropriate emergency management, leads to financial, structural, and human losses. the resulting loss depends on the capacity of the population to support or resist the disaster, their resilience.[1] this understanding is concentrated in the formulation: "disasters occur when hazards meet vulnerability".[2] a natural hazard will hence never result in a natural disaster in areas without vulnerability, e.g. strong earthquakes in uninhabited areas. the term *natural* has consequently been disputed because the events simply are not hazards or disasters without human involvement.[3] the degree of potential loss can also depend on the nature of the hazard itself, ranging from wildfires, which threaten individual buildings, to impact events, which have the potential to end civilization.

whore moans

sucking deep and paid handsomely or was it an ugly fucker that ripped me off and left me skint and a blowjob worse off. cheapskate. lips for sale, teeth included free of charge.

whore-moans

bite. damn! now my man will make me pay. marked. obviously you enjoyed it honey...."where exactly did that love bite come from?"

"hey it cost him two hundred i'll have you know"

"two hundred came without marks last time i checked slut."

your hands around my throat, surveying the damage. adds some more.

whore-moans.

crabs. jesus fucking christ almighty, you could saddle those bastards! i'm not going near you you dirty git. "you could just put a towel round there and do it anyway." you've got to be fucking joking. no. no way. taxi.

whore to control "that john's got the biggest fucking crabs you've ever seen...no, i left. call me later, yeah, bye."

control send in another whore. one whose eye isn't so keen. forty quid is forty quid. expendable product. bastards.

whore-moans

hotel room. bed. "oh baby i'm coming." whacks me round the face at the moment of cum. shit! what d'ya do that for? red. angry. sorry, sorry, sorry, so sorry...hurriedly fastens pants and shoves money in my hand...sorry sorry sorry....it's just...it's.....

aaah, fuck.....

whore-moans.

i just want to make you cum baby. an hour later. i just want to make you cum baby. you couldn't pay me enough honey. fake. aaaarrhr, aaarrhhh, oooh baby, yes, yes, that's right, yes, ooooohhhhhhhh. i made you cum....yeah right, sure you did. can i go now. no, i want you to stay, called up and paid an extra hour. we were having such fun. fuck.

whore-moans.

give me your ass sweetheart. i want your ass. don't do ass hun..sorry. i pay you good. you be like boy yes. look i told you...i. don't. do. ass. right. you go then. i want girl who like boy. boy good. girl okay. ass or no pay. fucking hell. been here an hour and no cash for it now. great. taxi. home. tired.

hotel. security. let you up if you come round here a second. free. shit. not again.

whore-moans.

turn off phone. hell. i'm a sperm bank lately. no more, no, can't do it.....tomorrow, yeah sure. sigh....

kerb crawler

the home office and police are clamping down on street prostitution with a new advertising campaign targeting kerb-crawlers...

the john slowed down. the girls were looking good tonight; there were lots of them out...strutting, hanging out, catching his eye. temptresses, every one of them. there was one who was particularly attracting his attention. the shortest of little black skirts, knee high socks (white), shiny black mary-jane shoes, white blouse, little back cardigan. mid twenties at a guess or maybe older...it was hard to tell in this light. probably older in his experience. you picked them up, drove somewhere, pulled up a skirt and it was then you could tell that a tom was older than she looked. either way, what she was selling he wanted to buy.

(advertisement)
the adverts will feature on local radio stations and carry warnings that kerb-crawlers could face arrest, a court appearance and warning letters to their home.

john's wife scrubbed the dishes on auto-pilot. fucking hell, that had been a hard day. the kids were really testing her recently, demanding, crying, fighting almost constantly. she'd no idea what had gotten into them; all she knew was that she was exhausted. she shoved a falling piece of her hair out of her eyes with a marigold wet hand. she felt really old lately; unattractive and old and it felt like months since she'd had sex, even wanted to, even thought about it....it must be hard for john, he was such a sweet husband, always there for her, never complaining. she felt terribly guilty about not fucking him. once, when they'd met, he'd told her he loved her sexual openness. now she felt as tight as a clam. dry, sexless, dull.

a £1000 fine and a driving ban, will also be mentioned.

john tried hard to ignore his growing debts. he didn't seem able to find a way out of it lately, so he just hid from it. his job in the haulage firm was all that kept things afloat really. thank fuck for small mercies he thought, laughing bitterly at the same time. god he hated that job, but at least it got him away from home, away from the kids endless whingeing, his wife's depression, the thought of his debts…..at least it was something.

the six week campaign is launched this week in london, middlesbrough, peterborough, southampton, bristol, bournemouth and leeds.

john wanted to move one day. manchester was okay but the beats were dead there now. cleaned up in the multi-agency drive to make the streets safe, the red light areas had all but disappeared and besides, living in the heart of one of the old areas meant he couldn't really pick up there; too much at stake. that old german bag might have died but there were always other busybody fuckers wanting to poke their noses into other people's affairs. he'd almost been caught out by that old bitch once. she'd flour-bombed his car then chased him down the road scratching his number plate onto her little pocket pad. the sad old witch. why couldn't she just watch telly for entertainment like most of the o.a.p.'s did round there.

no, if he could go anywhere, he'd try leeds he reckoned. lots of trees, nice and green...maybe cheer his wife up?

but the adverts face criticism from those who would like to see prostitution legalised and think such "draconian crackdowns" will drive sex workers underground.

stella re-applied her lippy and shoved the tatty old make-up bag back into her purse. fingering the condoms inside her handbag, she counted six (none of the punters would use them anyway out here) and they'd sat in her bag for a month or more now. plenty of trade, but condoms? no way missy! tenner or do without. no condoms it was then...she looked around her nervously. it was rough out here. she was no pussy but this 'beat' really scared her. two girls had been found dead only last month and the van that gave out rubbers and pins didn't come down here, it was stuck in a beat were there weren't even any more girls...service provider providing services to billy no-mates. fucking great! nowadays you couldn't even get a break when it was all too much. if it wasn't the crackpot fucking punters it was the nasty bastard pimps. lost...she felt fucking lost lately. an empty shell. any sense of family she had from meeting her mates or the workers on the van was gone. she felt alone. she carried a knife now but what good that would do if some psycho got hold of her she'd no idea. still...better to feel it in her purse and feel safer someway or other hey? a mate of hers had been to amsterdam last week; told her about the windows. 'fucking hell' she thought....'that'd be a right old cushty number. indoors, a bed, music if you wanted it, on full view so the psychos would be less likely to grab a girl there i bet.' she sighed....luxury she couldn't afford to think about really. this is how it was and she'd better just get on with it. bills needed paying. nothing else she could do in this fucking world anyway....this was her. this was stella.

the government hopes that clamping down on the demand for street prostitution will challenge the existence of street sex markets.

the government minister straightened his trousers and tucked his shirt back into his armani trousers. that one had been good. no complaints when he'd wanted to fuck her arse. less likely to get the clap that way he'd decided after one close shave when his wife nearly found out about his little habits. he'd discovered a leaking yellow pus from the end of his cock about a week after one particularly dirty looking whore had arrived from the agency one night. he'd been horny as hell and with no time to send her back (like he usually would) and demand someone more 'suitable.' 'i can do dirty' he'd thought. i'll give it a go. and he'd almost paid highly for it. a quick visit to the clap clinic and he'd sorted it all, hoping no-one would recognise him on his way in or out. got to be careful about these things; it wasn't long since that judge had lost his membership of the bar because of something similar. he'd changed agencies since then and things had calmed down again. he'd also reined in his occasional desire to go prowling the streets for the real dirty girls. too much at stake....

home office minister vernon coaker said: "local communities are fed-up with street prostitution - the sexual activity taking place in their parks and playgrounds, condoms and discarded needles littering the streets and innocent women mistakenly targeted and abused by men on the prowl."

innocent women/guilty women? fucking bitches the lot of them he thought as he prowled looking for his next target. she looked all right. she would do....bitch! yes...she would do nicely.

"for the residents it is intimidating, unpleasant and unsafe."

for stella, she was already dead. for john, he was about to lose everything. for john's wife....the prescription would need to be upped soon. for the minister – a good red and a steak for dinner he thought....that would do.....

for the residents, uninterrupted satellite t.v. and a pleasant view from the living room window would suffice.

the last taboo

lying in a pool of my own blood, some of it drying now, caked into little flaking bits of what would look like paint on my skin if you didn't know better. dry down my thighs, wet, red and dark; still running, between my legs. your sheets look like a massacre, your belly streaked with my blood and i could almost inhale the essence of it, metallic, mysterious. licking you i taste my blood, kissing you i become entranced. i've entered a place where i am you and you are me. writhing snake-like i want to climb inside you...you are inside me but i want more....i want to feel what it feels like to fuck me. i want to swap roles and genders for a moment and push, thrust and feel my muscles tight and hard, my belly taut. wombless. no tits.

but then i am back to myself, all cunt and curves. your sweat is mingling with mine now and my skin is sticky, my face red, my neck wet. deeper i go inside of myself; longing...remembering....no boundaries, no stopping, only flowing with a current like a wild river meandering where it will. you can't stop the force of that flow except with a dam that will always threaten to burst unless it deadens the nature of the water. my veins running rivers of wild water; flowing hot and still, swirling and deep, shallow as a sun-dried puddle in places, deeper than uncharted oceans in others. you kiss me and bring me back but then you carry on and take me away again. my lips, your lips; all one. no distinction.

i hungrily devour the taste of myself on you. my hands are red now too. my face streaked with blood yet? bodies as they were meant to be, as they should be...shameless, powerful, engaged, simple. my throat stifles a cry of longing. the words don't escape but the feeling is distilled all the more for their imprisonment.

the room was bathed in half light when we arrived there. tired, worn by the days' challenges, i just wanted to hold you, let you stroke my hair, rest, maybe talk a while. the gentle riffs of jay dilla sing out from your ipod, soothing my battered spirit. you pour me a whisky like you know i like it. straight, neat, one ice cube from time to time or none when i want the direct hit. today it's one and a splash of dry ginger which is a sure sign i'm exhausted otherwise i never mix my spirits, not whisky, but i'm thirsty, tired and fretting about something or other but i can't be bothered to work out what. the amber liquid trickles down my throat warming my whole body as it goes down and i release a huge sigh. you look at me quizzically; who is this woman you ask yourself and as i look into your deep brown eyes i ask myself the same question of you….who is this man? slowly the day ebbs away from me and i begin to shiver. i'm cold now, chilled with the day's change from full spring sunshine to that distinct cold born of the evenings when the clocks have only just gone back. it may be lighter but it isn't summer yet. weary i am…weary from the effort of holding so many people's expectations today. my son, his birthday, my daughters, their teenage desires, my ex husband and his confusions, me, my longing to be nothing more than who i am in the present moment. a simple short-term desire born of chaos.

men think little more than forty eight hours ahead. you told me this. you told me it goes something like this: when will i get fed, when will i sleep and when will i get laid? simple! that's it. and me, us women, how we take things into other dimensions with our creative wanderings, but there's a lot to be said for short term planning and so i borrow your philosophy and make it simple for myself too. baby, when will i get laid, will you feed me and can i sleep now please? you begin to lick my back and kiss my neck and my shattered body responds in spite of myself. i feel the heat rising and an energy starts to burn. you keep licking me; i'm on my belly and i feel my pubic bone crushed into the sheets wanting to grind a little now. mmmmmn, a murmur escapes my lips and encouraged maybe, you become more forceful. i feel your knee between my legs and suddenly you use the edge of your bones to flick my legs apart, holding me with the weight of your torso held tight above me. fuck you! you're always fighting to control me but you know you can't don't you baby? still, for this moment you're turning me on to fuck so i let it pass and wriggle beneath you, knowing i want to feel you force yourself inside me but you don't. instead you lay on top of me and the weight of you pushes me further into the bed and into submission. not yet tough baby…not yet…you see i can't let you feel for one moment that it's you who is in control. i'm training you, even in your forceful ways…i. am training. you. that's how it is and how it should be

.i could weep right now.

i will break every taboo with you and you just keep offering more. healing myself. knowing that sexual shame is a product of the perversion of our beautiful essence. no-one can tell me that this is wrong; that when i stop talking dirty with you, stop chaining your wrists to my bed, remove your blindfold, watch the marks fade….that i will be healed. no-one can tell me that when you stop calling me whore! or slut! or when you stop worshipping the seams on my nylons as they run along the back of my calf, across my knee, up my thighs and across my backside, that you will be healthy again. what measure of good health is this? whose? not mine for certain....

and as i lay back in my own bed this morning....watching the light send dancing polywashes of rainbow colour across my walls, listening to the birds sing, sunshine by 11am and the breeze blowing my curtains, i am reminded that in your acceptance and embracing of everything that makes us human, sexual beings, that nothing i could explore with you feels as though it is too much right now. pacing ourselves, pausing, integrating....i feel the disappearance of shame and in its place a glorious celebration of life. the last taboos will heal me.

the pantie drawer

she entered the dimly lit room and stopped a moment in the doorway. the half light scattered shadows across the bed and dappled the walls with monster shapes she'd have hidden from as a child.

"mummy, there's a crocodile under the bed!"

"no dear, the only monsters are in your imagination."

then i must have a big imagination mummy…

my robe flutters on the back of the door; i left it there last time i was here. slowly, my life becomes mingled with yours. my belongings indistinguishable soon if it weren't for the branding and stamping of identity. pink toothbrush. blue toothbrush. easy. my panties, your panties. not so easy.

i snuck in last week when you were at work and opened your bottom drawer looking for my nylons, the ones i'd left here last week and you know what i found. a drawer full of your goodies…porn mags, fetish dvds, sex toys, you know all the usual boy stuff, but then closer to the back and wrapped that little bit more tightly i found a plastic bag full of panties and they weren't mine.

at first i wasn't sure what to make of them. at first i detected the smell of fresh laundry and i'd expected them to be without any scent at all. only the smell of the plastic of the bag. that would have meant they were old, had been there for a while, but they smelled of perfume and soap flakes and on closer inspection, some even smelled of pussy only it wasn't my smell i could track there. so i stood a while and considered how i felt. i wanted to be angry with you and to storm out there and then. you never knowing i'd been there, you never knowing why i was acting all weird on you, me never saying. but in fact, try as hard as i could i just couldn't get mad. if you want to know the truth i was kind of intrigued in fact. did my boyfriend have a little obsession i didn't know anything about? had i just found his dirty little secret?

i touched them all one by one considering who wore panties like these. delicate cream net with pretty little pink embroidered flowers. brightly coloured polka dots on white cotton. sheer, lace trimmed, palest pink fabric. mine were mostly black so this feast of colour intrigued me. they were bigger than i would wear; women of generous hips must have worn them once. i held one pair to my cheek and imagined you fucking their owner whilst i spied on you. you would see me right at the last moment and i would hold your eye as you shot your cum into that wide-hipped woman. i would smile and walk away which would confuse you.

so now i was back at your bedroom door and you were behind me. we enter your room and i am tense with the knowledge of your secret. you don't know i know about it and the thought is suspended between us like new sex.

i am about to bring your pantie drawer into our sex.

pissed

pub. menstrual bleeding. can men smell it? do men know it?

drugs. got some. burning holes in my pocket. longing to do it now. longing to let go. longing.....

sex. "i like your dress. i'd like to remove it." "been so long i've forgotten what it is mate." "you're wild, i'm gonna miss you." "you can't go...you didn't sit on my knee."

men. can't shop. carry the cards. what else is there? don't even know their own kitchens. masculine. feminine. merged. emasculated. feminised. fucked.

work. blah blah blah. not important. bitch bitch curse.

writing. eurudice. my cunt talks. ela has the tightest cunt in the world. yet, in real life, every blessing is also a curse.

where can i get a copy of this genius book? cunt. my cunt was smoking on a chat show once.

green dress. i like your green dress. green eye shadow. i like your green eye shadow. i like you. some people are ruined in some places. sometimes you gotta get out.

whisper. she was wrong.

fucked. my sister's husband fucked her over. my husband fucked me over. i lied.

texts. precision required.

kids. handed over my life mate.

kids. teenage. me? yeah....

jd would be good. thanks doll.

no i understand. it's a long drive.

then there were horses and blood and love and lust and shootings and more whisky and shit i can't be arsed taking off my make-up now i wonder if i'll get spots aah fuck it!

bed

pissed

a snapshot. my life as it is today.

books. scattered everywhere. my life full of words. language twists through my brain almost constantly at present. i love words. i'm losing the ability to capitalise and punctuate correctly in this heady new love affair with words. spellcheck? no thanks...too busy. words. my favourite word right now is 'cunt.' how juvenile. how puerile. how delicious...

records. scattered everywhere. music coming into my life. my sweet love brings music to me. he turns his vinyl and rocks his body and soul. music saved his life. it's growing mine. ever fallen in love with someone ever fallen in love with someone ever fallen in love with someone you shouldn't have fallen in love with?

the postman pulls up in a silver people carrier fancy car like you've never seen. what happened to walking and bikes. the postman. anything for me? a book? a record? a love letter?

bags. full of bits of my life. red leather. a satin blindfold. lubricant. condom. books (obviously). pens, scraps of paper. black and white films waiting to be developed: remind me of other snapshots. moments already lived. done. bags containing bits of me everywhere. can i leave one at yours next time. hold it. hold me. just a quiet corner. subtle. gradual. tentative. fucking glorious.

art. paintings. photographs. cards. on every wall. in every space.

shit! my house is becoming crazy.

i'm in transition. transforming. clear it out. get rid of the old me to celebrate the bones of the new me. dance? yeah okay.....you put on the dub and let's disappear again.....

i fucking love you. i fucking love my life. i fucking know shadows. i fucking shake their hands, spit on them and then dance with them. my language is terrible. my mother would blush.

friends...come with me and dance a while.

dance like your heart will crack open and out with the bats, and the rats and the lyrics. out with the spells and the drugs and the love. out with the hope and the despair and the faith. faith for the faithless. hope for the hopeless. dreams for the emptied. vacant lot for rent. life

fight

i went and sat in the corner of the room, your room, snarling like a hungry panther.

"fuck off" i yelled at you..."you. fuck. off." again, in case you didn't get it first time round.

you look at me and carry on with what you're doing, as if you hadn't heard me which just makes me mad, so i start pacing the room, looking for a way in, or a way out.

"you know what...you fuck me right off" i stated, as if it that would be the one that would turn you on to me. personalise my 'fucking off,' use it more as 'it's *you* that fucks me off,' rather than 'you fuck off' and maybe you'd hear me. you start singing to yourself and that pisses me off even more....not because you're ignoring me but because you can't sing.

"baby....you know before, when you were fucking me...well....did you cum?" you ask me. and i stare at you viciously. you bastard.

"did *you*?" i ask, your cum dripping down my thigh.

"you know i did honey" you state. you're puzzled by my tone, i can tell. you're unaware of where this come from, my festering desire to pick a fight; i'm still looking for an escape route.

"you just don't get it do you?" i ask. you don't get it one tiny little bit. you fuck, you cum, you sing to yourself, you're happy. your balls are emptied and a longing is quelled and nothing else matters, but i'm sinking into myself here and i don't know how to get out. picking a fight seems as good a lifebelt as any.

"i'm going to see x tomorrow" i tell you, knowing he irritates the hell out of you. "he's doing so much right now you know and it's pretty exciting stuff. i wanna get into some of that, you don't mind do you baby?"

"nah" you say and carry on with your cooking and fucking singing.

it's like boxing in a dream this is. every time i land a punch my fist goes through you and yet you're there still, smiling at me, facing up to me. once in a dream i tried to beat you to a pulp and all i got was sore arms from never being able to hit you but i never stopping trying. i probably ran and ended up naked in a public place or busy street if my dreams were running true to form. can everyone see me when i'm doing this? has everyone got me pegged or is it just you?

fucker.

i begin to curl up on your leather chair. i pull that baby blue fleece blanket over myself and admit to myself that i'm going to go hungry tonight on the fight front. you come over and stroke my hair....

"fancy a fuck?" you ask me.

"yeah" i say, and we go to bed.

training

1. dark. brooding. intense. fucking riled. strange. irritated. confrontational. you fucking what? yeah right. try it. what-eh-vah. naaaaaah. right now. right here. come on then. lick my injuries. bring me your ass. bring me my belt. bring me off. right here. right now. no words. action. no excuses. action. nothing but action. no explanation. no offerings. no uncertainty. action. just do it. do it now. bring me your love. bring it whimpering and screaming on a silver platter dripping with blood. let a murder of crows hover around waiting for their moment. let the rattlesnake's tail sing loud in her rage. bring me your love. bring it now. stop telling me of this and that and the things i don't need to know and never asked you about. stop telling me about this and that and the fucking other. bring me my belt. my whip will do. bring me your ass. your back will do. sting. scream. bite. weep. wail. whore. be careful. the whore you see now is not the whore you imagined then. the whore you imagined then is the whore you see before you now. you want me? lick my injuries.

2. long, sharp, evil looking. my nails. red, pale, brownish. my lipstick changes according to my mood and if i were to go out tonight, it would be red as fresh blood. angry and jarring, scarred and fresh

3. i keep my nails done and my hair coloured and well cut at all times. when not working the system job, i always wear heels and i have a fondness for stockings, nylons and panties. corsets are good. you can't see my

switch under a corset. the whalebone conceals the hard edges.

4. when i finish the system work this week, i'm leaving my 'work shoes' behind as a kind of waving goodbye. a legacy gesture. a permanent departure. practical is over rated. those shoes. someone can have them. they're not shiny enough, or sexy enough and it irritates the hell out of me to put them on. i want black patent leather and heels, all zips and buckles.

5. to unwind i would crank up the volume and dance wildly to the cramps.
plugged in. underworld. kmfdm. nick cave. the klaxons. anything loud and fast and furious. anything that makes me sweat. i can do that. get drunk on whisky. take a whip or belt to a submissive. take them to total submission. sweet. submission. sweet. surrender. really hard. fuck. rip tights.

6. the mistress paced the floor, flicking the end of her crop into the open palm of her hand. occasionally the tip would sting upon contact and she would smile an evil smile of recognition. i know what this feels like she thought and i whimper about it far less than he does. no mercy. training and no mercy. "my terms or nothing" she declared aloud to herself. no mercy she thought, grinding her cigarette butt under the spike heel of her patent black boots, deep, deeper into the wooden floor boards with a malice usually reserved for her less capable subs.
her mind was busy; agitated and slightly pissed off. she was dangerous in this mood. her darker

machine nature had an innate tendency to fester when she was displeased and though admittedly there were times when she searched for reasons to be displeased but this was not one of them. seven tasks; two incomplete. a third completed and then relapsed. she was testing him and he was failing, over and over. a human lover was one thing, a human submissive another. if he desired both, he needed to meet both ends of the deal; no compromise.

    register 690983093 had not yet fully understood the implications of this ownership. he required further training. the mistress was going to make sure he got it. machine whore. she flicked the switch and became automaton: it was easier that way. the blood drained and her veins filled with anti-freeze as she made the transition. her telephone auto-dialled her submissive....

gregor

fishnet stockings. seams. delicately rising. thigh. warm. sticky. hot now. rising. seam stops at beautifully curved buttock. buttock raising. swelling. full of promise. hint of lace. edges. panties. frills. sensual heat. you trace a tongue up the back of my leg....biting slightly at the top. wet.

skirt. tight. panties. seen. so tight it impeded my walk. heels. high. shiny. click click. heels. beautiful.

body. all curves and sinews. dresses. lipstick. perfume. heels. girls. woman. you wish......

neck. kiss neck. bite neck. throat. sound. moan.......bite.......

boy. willing. tongue hanging at thought of licking. pussy. pussy. pussy. lost. sensual dreams of faraway places. pussy. pussy. pussy. lick lick lick. please me. go on. do it now. fuck me. go on. do it now. hold me. go on. do it now. lost. holding. locked. tight tight tight.

mistress. sharp. cunning. fever. need. tense. uncertain. slightly anxious you. where will she take me this mistress? home. inside. home. deep .deeper. lost. found. home.

a look. a glance. a moment......shared. alone. solitary. yearning. desiring of more. desiring of solitude. desiring of unity. desiring of every goddam thing! craving. love. craving pleasure. craving lust. craving. deep. deep. love.

eyes. meet me. eyes. see me. eyes. know me. and then howl at the moon.

"fuck off you bitch...just....fuck......off..............."
lost. found.
home
love

metamorphosis

the first drop of whisky hit her lips. the woman, who was dressed entirely in white and feeling very 'soft' this evening, let the warm, hot, familiar taste soothe her…take her back to landscapes well travelled.

"jesus, i needed that!". her friend stared at her:

"claudia, will you *ever* stop that? you know it's really not doing you any favours don't you babe?"

"fuck off julia! just fuck off with your righteous judgment hey. let's not go there tonight. i feel a bitch of a mood coming on and i don't want to fall out with you, but push me and i might just do that…"

"you know what, you're impossible lately don't you? everything is just sex and drugs and rock and roll with you isn't it? what about work, responsibility, commitment; what about love? what about just reining it in for a while and trying out life like the rest of us live it?"

"oooh, well put it like that baby…"

"oh, fuck off claudia. just fuck off"

claudia was happy. for the first time in years she felt really happy and quite frankly her happiness disturbed her, because she was more accustomed to unhappy. her happiness fucked with her head. her happiness threatened everything. it rode in on a silver and black low-rider harley davidson, stereo blasting, sun on skin, too few clothes…her happiness disturbed her because it was born of a devilishly selfish lust for living and this was far more destabilizing than a misery born of longing for change. the misery had fit like an old glove and other people had recognised it, courted it and tried to soothe it. they stroked it, communicated in earnest with it and tried to 'cure' it. they were reassured by it. her friends felt safe with it. other people couldn't cope with her happiness. they tried to contain it, squash it, reject it, deny it…..

"fill my glass while you're up would you babe"

"fill it your fucking self claudia, and then go try to remember you're (fill in age) why don't you…."

"oh yeah right, sorry, forgot. pass me the bottle then would you? you can't object to passing me the fucking bottle…surely?"

the two friends sat glowering at one another. you are this. i am that. i am this. you are that. bridges in between them…burnt. almost down to ashes.

"you wanna try pole dancing with me next week hun?"

"you really don't get it do you claudia"

"what?"

"aaah fuck it…forget it….and no, i don't want to pole dance with you. how about line dancing? isn't that more 'age appropriate ' (sarcasm)"

"well now babe (sarcasm exchanged)…if i ask you nicely would you swap my negligee for a nightie? exchange my dildo for condom? swap my naughty, angry lover for a dickless liberal leftie? swap my phone sex for an answering machine? swap my stilettos for sensible shoes? swap my cunt for a vagina?"

"there's no talking to you lately claudia….i'm going"

"shut the door behind you would you babe"

the two friends parted for the evening, not sure when they would see each other again.

scars

sometimes i like to gaze at my scars and pick at them a while. faded, angry, some still red and running deeper, they are like old friends. familiar and comfortable. scabby and safe. i know them. i know how they got there and what i felt like before they became scars...when they were still wounds.

you come along and stare at my scars. i'm staring at your scars.

they must like each other; they blush. i think your scars are fascinating and they make me feel like a girl; tiny and obscure, powerless and unknowing.

i don't know about your scars, i only know my own. my scars would like to hang out with your scars; fuck a while, chat over whisky, read the odd newspaper together, probably in bed and then doze until there is something more urgent or compelling to do.

my scars are harder than your scars. your scars are bigger than my scars.

my scars want to take on your scars behind the bike sheds. 'don't bring yer mates and leave yer ciggies on the floor over there. i'm having them when i've battered your scars.'

my scars can be perverse little bastards sometimes. they want to suck the marrow out of you and replace it with dripping mango juice and papery physalis. they want to see tiny champagne bubbles popping through your veins. they like to tear at warm ciabatta and shovel fat olives into your mouth, smell the coffee grinds on the stove and then clear the kitchen table with one smooth arm movement so that they can fuck you on it...here...now!

occasionally they get bigger than their boots though and start driving me, telling me what to do, try to pick a fight or two. they become dark and shadowy, and they spit and curse like a wizened old voodoo priestess.

watch out! you don't want to cross them when they're like that...but i do try so hard to reign them in and keep them under control.

my scars.

horseradish and mayonnaise

jesus christ! is every experience with you an erotic one?

sainsbury's. 11.00am. i need to do my shopping but i don't have a car. you have a car. you take me. blushing (i've never shopped with you before and it's perversely intimate don't you think...shopping together?), blushing, i shove in my pound and take a trolley. i walk into the bright neon-lit store; daytime shoppers, a fair number of suits. it's the posh bit of town though once it was home to ordsall parade and that wasn't posh; that was all graffiti and hoodies, wire mesh fronted shops and 'dangerous' youths. but now, suits, yes, and quite a few browsing mums, looking for daytime entertainment to pass the toddler filled moments no doubt. i've been there, shopping was fun, a distraction. but not like this.

you come up behind me as i'm filling my flimsy veg bags with apples and whisper something filthy in my ear. i feel my cheeks hot and my cunt wet.

i'm in sainsbury's.

i move on and you say "sweetie, remind me i need mayonnaise" and i say "sweetie, remind me i need horseradish." his and hers. if we were animals we'd be spraying our piss around each other right now...

i have a really tight skirt on and you can see my panty line and i know that turns you on. aisle seventeen; tinned goods and you grind your cock into my backside as i reach forward to get a tin of beans. i say "3 'o' clock, your right, blonde in a mackintosh and high heels." you say "i know baby, i've seen her. that's quite a good look." and you carry on grinding yourself into me and you bite my neck. security passes the end of the aisle and i straighten my skirt and move on. i'm in sainsbury's.

nylons and panties next....oh jesus, there's no chance now! you buy me some, we get home and rip open the packets and i put them on. they look so pretty. so clean and so 'nice.' cotton panties, natural tan tights. gusset marked out in slightly denser thread. you grab my cunt through the nylons and the panties and tell me it's hot, that you can feel the heat coming from me.

i want you badly now and you want me. you tear at my tights and pull down my panties just enough to be able to fuck me hard whilst you look at them. i've filled your dirty mind with a fantasy i invented five minutes ago and you cum like a greedy bastard. we wrap ourselves around each other, sweaty and spent.

sainsbury's. what a turn-on that was.

sleep

i slept with *those* panties, my own cum filled panties besides my head last night. the smell of them turned me on, made me want you even more. i buried my face in them, inhaled their glorious stink over and over, addicted to the remembering they stirred in me. i love the smell of your cum. is that really fucking perverse baby? is it? should i just go get a teddy bear?

pretty pale blue cotton with tiny cherries printed all over them, they were brand new yesterday, dirty as hell by four p.m. god that was good...i'm such a cock slut for you! but you know it, and you want me too. pussy whore! you want me over and over and i want you over and over. reaching, grasping, yearning, longing.....

i crawl into my bed, my eyes heavy, my head muddled slightly by the warmth of my whisky and i think about you. i can't think about you for long, though or i get too turned on and if i'm honest, start to get all lovey-dovey too and that won't do. i'm not going to do that....

"what if you break down my barriers and then leave me in a jelly-like heap, all mess and madness?"

"what if you open me up and then walk away?"

challenged not to judge you, or to fear you, or to contain you (but that bit is easy actually), i stare long and hard at you. "listen you fucker, i fucking love you" i want to say. should you tell a person you love them like that? aren't you supposed to say it over dinner with wine and roses, or in bed, whilst 'making love.' but we don't do dinner and wine or making love. we savour food like hungry pigs and we fuck.

and i love it.

blood

the woman licked the blood that was trickling from the wound on her forearm. it was starting to dry up a little now…she rather enjoyed the taste though, and was sorry to think it would probably stop bleeding soon.

staring out of the window, the rain fell in heavy fat droplets down the pane and onto the windowsill, where it pooled, still, in its resting place just within her view. relentless rain. relentless pain.

she had fought with her lover the previous afternoon. what had started as wild fucking had turned into a proper fight. dark, brooding, competitive. that was the thing that got to her…the competition. he'd started losing it and so he'd hit her. the blood had trickled slowly from the side of her lip and she just blinked, rubbed the back of her hand across her mouth, stared at the red streak across her skin and left.

that's when she realised she enjoyed the taste of the blood.

today she had gone back and asked him to use the knife on her. she trusted him…ironically…..pathetically? either way, she wanted him. he looked at her. considered her request for about, oh, let's see…one minute, and then agreed.

she walked slowly over to the bed and lay across the counterpane, spread-eagled, already gone somewhere else. she was offering herself….

"what will you do baby?"

that was the only dialogue exchanged between them.

he opened the drawer besides the bed and took out a laguiole hunting knife he'd actually bought for her the previous year for her birthday. they were good french knives; sharp, functional blades. she looked at it and smiled. it was perfect. she'd used it twice before. once to cut some testy vines from the underside of her car that had become tangled on their way through some spanish wilderness or other, and once to skin the three foot snake her friend had brought to her, already dead, last month.

she breathed deeply and surrendered. he sat on the edge of the bed and took the knife in his right hand and made the smallest incision upon her forearm. she winced and he leaned over and kissed her. they fucked and she came wildly and with more noise and passion than she, or he, expected. the cut bled more than you'd have imagined and was still bleeding when she left, shortly after they had dressed and continued with their respective days.

the pool of rain forming on her windowsill was making her horny again; the relentless nature of it driving her into darker and darker depths.

she thought of her lover, picked up a pen and a sheet of pristine white note paper, and wrote:

"even though you already exist, i invented you. i ate you once before you were born and then spat you out again. you were all bitter tasting and toxic. you were all bones and tendon, ligament and tight, tight muscle. i wanted flesh, blood, heart... so i spat you out. you became very sinuous as a child and went off dancing at the age of three. i imagine you're still dancing now but i've learned to live with my loss....."

sincerely,

cara.

"tom"

could he see her as quite remarkable? vast, cavernous, fascinating, wide open? or tight, knotted, closed? did it matter anyway? what difference did it make to the day to day running of her life? none! none whatsoever, which meant of course that she was free to do exactly as she pleased in any given moment, and since every moment was all that mattered, well, damned if he did and damned if he didn't!

as she slowly and gently finished sewing the wound in his arm, he winced in pain despite her tenderness. the vodka he'd liberally applied to both his injury and himself had taken the edge off the sting of the jarring newness of the knife laceration, and helped to dull the confusion a little but it wasn't enough. besides, the confusion he was feeling was also serving to magnify his awareness of the surreal nature of this scene.

half an hour earlier he had staggered, bloody and on the verge of shocked tears, into their apartment. clutching his arm to stem the flow of the blood (she would curse him if he ruined the carpets), he simply let himself in and sat in the big leather chair in the corner by the window, breathing deeply, trying to steady himself and make sense of what had happened. she was in the shower; she would be working then…..

no police. no involvement.

he walked over to the kitchen drawer and took out her sewing kit, opened the cupboard and removed the screw cap top from the vodka and slugged hard. the neat, hot liquid calmed him. methodically (surprising under the circumstances), he picked out a strong thread and as sharp a needle as he could find; both strong enough to stitch through flesh. grimacing at the thought of what he was about to do, he held his cigarette lighter under the needle, flicked on the flame and ran the violet blue core of it over the length of the needle until it was black. charcoal soot coated black. he then wiped the needle on the corner of his shirt (well cut, brown cotton, gold buttons) until he felt fairly sure that the needle was as sterile as could be expected and was necessary for the job of piecing together his own torn skin.

black; he chose black thread.

it took him several moments to thread the needle his hands were shaking so badly. he needed to act soon before the wound started to coagulate and make his job tougher than it already was. standing on the kitchen floor (tiled), he generously poured the vodka over the wound now. additional sterilising wouldn't go amiss seeing as he'd no idea what kind of blade, or what state it had been in, had been used to slash his upper arm. everything had happened so fast and whilst on the surface it had seemed to all intents and purposes a random attack, he knew it wasn't. it was something to do with her, but he'd no idea what. into what realms she strayed when she wasn't with him he didn't even begin to imagine. he'd long since got used to that. she was totally silent about her work; about her life outside of their flat. it had become a kind of unspoken law that he wouldn't ask......

"don't ask me the questions if you don't want to know the answers", she'd warned him early on in their relationship. sometimes he wanted to know the answers, and though it pained him not to ask, especially when she came in pissed or stoned or freaky, he would bite his lip and restrain himself. far greater than his fear of the answers was his fear of losing her if he pushed her too far.

"all you need to know baby, is that when i'm there, i'm not 'me'…'kay?" though her rhetorical question did not require an answer from him. it was more of a statement of fact. accept it or leave. he chose to accept.

'when i'm with *you* i'm not me' he would imagine her saying. it bothered him that it felt like the truth somehow, but he loved her and so he accepted all of it; everything, without question.

he slugged once again on the vodka. not too much or he'd be pissed and mess up the stitching. with a deep breath, on the exhale, he pushed the needle into his flesh and heard someone howl…

"jesus christ almighty! fuck! fucking hell! bastard. motherfucking. cunt!," at which point she appeared.

"what the fuck do you think you're doing tone?" (she always called him tone and most of the time he loved it, it usually meant she was in a good mood but something didn't fit now and it irritated the hell out of him. before he could stop himself…

"oh…well….what the fuck does it *look* like i'm doing baby?

he regretted it the moment the words escaped his lips. even now, in this ridiculous situation, *he* was taking care of *her* needs, her moods.

"listen you sarcastic bastard, you're standing there stitching up your own arm. you pop out to get ciggies from the shop and you come back bloody, seemingly half pissed and sewing up your own fucking arm and you think my question warrants your sarcasm? well fuck you tone! tell you what, why don't i get you a little patch for that so you can make the job a bit prettier hey?" and she turned and walked back into the bathroom, slamming the door behind her.

the bitch! the fucking bitch! she didn't even wait to hear his answer. worse, he could feel the urge to run after her, whilst sewing, to explain.

"baby...don't be like that" he pleaded, "c'mon, you know i love you baby."

silence.

"baby...open the door"...ouch! jesus that fucking hurt. the needle, thread now locked into the first stitches was dangling from the wound whilst he tried to persuade her to come out. if she left for work now, she wouldn't come back tonight. he knew how she operated.

"baby..."

"my fucking name is stella! ok tone....got it? my fucking name is stella! now what d'you want. i'm late already!"

"look stella, some cunt attacked me down there. that little road...you know, the one between earl's court station and here? busy as fuck and the chancy bastard just swiped me in broad daylight. he knew he wanted me. it was meant for me. i've no idea what's going on stella but if i call the cops they'll be all over you like a rash, so that's why i'm doing a fucking d.i.y job stella. so you don't have to go to the cells for a night and come home stinking of pig food and disinfectant again."

the door clicked open. she didn't come out but it was a start......

he went in. stella was sitting on the toilet seat. stockings, matching panties and bra (his favourites), pulling her red dress on over her head. god he loved her in that! her heels lay beside her, the last thing before she left. he wanted to kick them away so that she couldn't go.

"c'mere baby" she said softly.

as he noved towards her he felt the adrenalin that'd been keeping him able to do this job, the sewing of his arm, slowly leaving his bloodstream and with it all of his bravado. he dropped to his knees.

"fucking hell stell…what's going on baby, i don't get it.…"

"sssssshhhhhhh" she crooned.

"i can't do it baby. i can't sew it. it hurts like a bitch! must've been a rusty blade too cos it's throbbing like fucking mad now honey. "

"give it to me. i'll do it baby", and she kissed him. a long slow lingering kiss. deep, feeling, tender, turned on in an instant and all was well again in his world. stella stroked his arm just below the wound (which made him incredibly nervous). he flinched and gave her a half smile.

a love story...

she paced the room ferocious as ever. her heels click click clicking on the wooden floorboards, laminated, highly polished, beautiful. she flicked her ash onto them, looked down at them scornfully, and then ground the still lit butt into the floor beneath her...

"fake! i hate fake!" she spat.

they were looking over the new house, pondering the all mirrored walls and the proximity of the neighbours.

"sweetie, come over here and let me hold you, i need your gorgeous self next to me."

there was no question that he would refuse her.

earlier that day he had run errands for her; heeled her boots, taken her clothes (soiled with his own ejaculations) to the dry cleaners, made her lunch, helped her sort out her administration and planning, and then fucked her hard, the way she liked it, across his kitchen table. then they had gone to see the house.

she disarmed him; made him feel open, alive, peaceful, capable. he softened her; tore down her barriers and created a heartbeat she'd not recognised in herself for quite some time now. she felt strong, powerful, loving. he felt all manner of things.

she was becoming ferocious about protecting him; about protecting their two hearts which lay all bloody, ripped and open on the floor between them. catlike she prowled, eyes flickering over any intruders, assessing, sizing up...

"shall i devour them, play with them, or just sniff them and leave them be?" she would ask herself. sniff, sniff, sniff....

and he would drop to his knees, lost in the face of great things.

lost in the face of love.

there was often no need for words between them; their love was a life-form growing independently of them or so it seemed to her.

always leaving him as much space as she needed for herself.

she bit at his neck, savouring him. he tore at her clothes, greedy for her. she licked his face, his head, his body, all the way down his belly, past his navel, to the waistband of his trousers. she never seemed to tire of him. always wanting more....wanting to climb inside him.

"fuck me" she said.

he heard himself screaming somewhere. she disappeared.

pimp

"she pays me back with pity, the basest coin of all" ~ barton fink.

i rise, beaten and empty, and smash the teeth from your fucking mouth. the end of the metal mixing with the taste of the blood on your crushed lip. you look pretty like that, the pattern of the bruise already beginning to form across your cheek and forehead. you look shocked. you weren't expecting it.

i approach you now, you dirty scumbag. pitiful and low, cowardly and weak. you don't know how strong i am. you underestimated me. i am powerful beyond your dreams. you are powerful in your small world of beggars and thieves…no-one questions you there until the money arrives. then class comes into the hierarchy of villainy. you are beneath my contempt. you are nothing. you were emptied long before i was, only i have something left. you have nothing. dead.

i cannot judge you these days. pity you…i pity you. i've lost my judgment. i've lost my hate. i'm happy to part with them. they were a pain up the arse frankly. fair weather friends…there one minute, gone the next, then back again with a hand out for a loan or something.

once you thought you were big. big and strong. forceful and terribly clever but you always had less wits than me. had i chosen your end of the profession, i'd have retired wealthy a long time ago…no-one much the poorer.

but you….you stand before me now begging my forgiveness but i don't have any to give you. the christians will tell me that my lack of forgiveness will eat me alive but they would be wrong. my lack of forgiveness sustains me. it's my judgment was eating me alive. i will never forgive you and i'm comfortable with that. pious gods have no place in my passions or my healing.

    you don't appear to have a god. faithless.

    i would loan you mine but s/he is busy smashing your teeth out right now.

transformation

the woman looked her nemesis in the eye. it was currently laid out on the tiled floor of her bathroom. she wasn't sure how it had gotten there. it was writhing about seeking either sympathy or pain relief and she wasn't sure which of those either. its skin was damp and cold to the touch; perhaps moist would have been a more accurate description. moist, tepid, damp, repellent, fetid, foul smelling, slimy and extremely ugly, and it had dogged her for years....

she looked at it now, all wart-skin and bruises, pock marks and crater-like indentations where once it had been beautiful...maybe....well, capable at the very least. it had held her, seduced her, intrigued her, it had even made love to her on numerous occasions and yet now, it was reduced to this pathetic squirming mess in front of her.

"you're messing up my bathroom" she stated.

squeak, squeak, squeak. not even capable of words these days and worthy only of her contempt. she looked closer at the creature; there was something struggling behind its eyes, something trying to break out or just die.

she left it there and marched into her bedroom. it'll not be going anywhere for a while she thought....too weak....

she took a bag and began the herculean task of jettisoning the majority of her belongings.

transformation.

she looked upon her things as a child may look upon something it has never countered before...puzzled, 'were they ever mine?' 'did i ever like them?' 'why did i buy them?' a million questions forming as she put the things into a large black dustbin liner. ruthless...she'd been carrying them all around with her for fucking years.

examples: - there was a buddha statue in gold, holding a small disc stating simply 'faith'. i had faith when i found myself whoring on queensway and mayfair, fucking in strangers' cars on dangerous patches of wasteland, no-one knowing where i was, or whether i would return. i had faith when the fist landed in my face and i thought i was dead, she thought. she binned the buddha.

there were trinkets; a disk of painted stained glass with a poppy design in a deep blood red. why do i need to stare at a poppy on a glass? i looked poppies in the eye when i found myself puking up on a train station platform, legs barely able to carry me, sweat dripping from every part of me, parts i never even knew could sweat. i knew poppies then, she thought. she binned the stained glass disc.

there were crystals and little wooden drawers filled with the odds and ends of a life she once lived. she was living it only last month in fact only suddenly it didn't belong to her. she scraped them all up in one motion of her arm and swept them into the bag. gone.

handbags, belly dancers decorative hip ties, net curtains covered in roses, heart shaped baskets from her wedding...maybe not that....oil burners, incense holders, earthenware pots, collected stones, empty whisky bottles, photograph frames holding pictures she no longer cared for, broken fabric flowers, papers and files of no importance or consequence, a jar of her children's first teeth...no not that...wicker baskets filled with small mementoes that she no longer needed in order to piece together her sense of herself, a plethora of meaningless gifts bestowed upon her when people could find no other last minute christmas presents. she'd kept them all...regardless of their significance; some *because* of their significance. now everything had suddenly changed and she wasn't sure why. something was trying to get out....she thought it may have looked like the thing in the bathroom.

she carried on now...focused with the drive of a strange unformed objective. throw. everything. out. start from scratch....start afresh....don't hold on...freefall. she could hear the call of the falcon in the distance and she dropped to her knees to return the high pitched squeal of her heart's calling.

"come for me baby" she murmured, "come for me..."

her eyes were running a river now; flowing freely in big fat goblets of emptying pain.

"you know what....fuck it!" she said aloud, sweeping every fucking thing into the bag. take a chance...from nothing, everything is born. from point zero; from total annihilation and destruction comes bittersweet creation.

when everything had gone, she lay down and slept. her dreams were dark that night. nothing left. obliteration. she dreamt she was in that place again, the strange landscape she had visited so often in her dreams. the street was wide, exceptionally wide. contemporary, stark, and yet something like a ghost town in the 'feel' of it....like a scene in an old deserted spaghetti western scene only with a post-modern twist. dust balls blew in the wind. there was no-one else here. no-one else inhabited this place. it felt so familiar to her...some kind of home. she looked around her in her dreaming state.

"this place is not my home" she said....and she vanished.

back into sleep she sank deeper and deeper into some tunnel this time; an alice in wonderland tunnel of fleeting images, strange people, flashing moments, memories...

the queen of hearts yelled "off with her head," and alice shouted

"oh fuck off will you, you stupid bitch!"

her heart was beginning to beat so hard she felt a panic attack coming on. 'oh shit i'm gonna die down here she thought. in the middle of all of these freaks and gangstas, i'm gonna die?' rising very fast back up the tunnel now, it was this sensation that was causing her heart to beat faster. not panic but freedom. not death but liberation.

when she woke, she was drenched in sweat. her bedclothes were tangled around her torso and she couldn't move her left arm. dead. she'd fallen asleep on it and now it didn't belong to her. she lay flat on her back and breathed. there was no sound. the creature in the bathroom had silenced. where the fuck was that thing now?

moving slowly towards the bathroom door she gently pushed it open with the foot of an extended leg. nothing. she peered around the door. empty. in the corner, just next to where she had left the sorry thing, a note. a note written on a curled up piece of tatty old newsprint...

"when you stopped needing me i had to leave. i will always love you. i have poisoned you, but i loved you. i have strangled you, but i loved you. i have lied to you, fucked your friends, imprisoned you once or twice and battered you with my fists on more than one occasion and always you came back to me. i abused you both physically and sexually. i abused you emotionally, mentally and verbally and always you came back to me. i loved you with more depth than anyone you have ever known. my passion was unrivalled by anyone or anything you have ever seen or come across, but now you no longer need me, i am unable to survive. i fucked you over and you came for me. you won…sincerely ----"

    she wept, and turned to her lover who was lying beside her.

    "did you hear that baby? did you hear any of that?" she fancied it had been spoken out loud but it was in fact, a silent dialogue.

    she had loved that beast.

    it was gone.

    she slept in the arms of her lover.

the overwhelming human desire to be loved

love…you capitalise on my overwhelming human desire to be loved. i'm fifteen; you fuck my best friend and then come back to me, all covered in love bites and dripping with the stink of her pussy on your face. i kiss your cheek and recoil, repelled by what i could smell there, but i smile at you and forgive you, so you went and did it again about one hour later.

i'm sixteen. you ask me to keep watch while you rob that office. i love you and so i agree. when you're in styal jail about three months later, i risk my family for you and leave home, choosing you over them. i never went back.

i'm seventeen…you spot me in a nightclub. you're cool, i'm naïve. you turn up at my flat one morning dripping blood from a gaping wound in your fist. you'd put it through someone's door, and then tried mine. "you could use the bell" i say and you grasp your bleeding hand and reply "you could fucking get me a drink…now….baby," and i do. i love you and i choose to ignore all of my friends yelling 'psycho, psycho, psycho' in my ear. i leave for the bright lights and the big city with you and before you know it i'm whoring for you, fucking you on demand, being imprisoned by you, breaking contact with everyone i know for you, begging you, terrified of you.

i'm eighteen…still with you, unable to leave until i find my moment. i run, and then she tells you where i'm hiding. you come hunting for me. knife. threats to your livelihood cannot go unchecked. i'm cleverer than you though and i make my second escape in as many days. gone.

i'm nineteen. you sweet talk me into your service. all snakeskin shoes and feather hats, silk coats and well cut suits. "you know you're my number one girl don't you baby?" "you know we will be good together don't you?" and i say "yes," blindly and sweetly and foolishly. i loved you beyond measure. i loved dancing lovers rock with you in dark, smoky early morning clubs. i loved waking up next to you in our notting hill flat. then one night you didn't come home and my necklace had disappeared. i saw it the next day round another woman's neck and i wept for my loss. you had gone though you were still there with me, the outline of you at least.

i'm twenty one and on the run. jails; i'd do anything for you. i put myself at risk over and over just so you'll love me the way i want to be loved. you don't. you love me the only way you know how. a couple more years then i leave. it's the hardest thing i've ever done.

twenty three. i've met you again. i've known you since i was fifteen. you want to 'help' me. take me away from all this. i let you. i leave and i'm sick for quite some time. it's then that i discover your love has conditions. there are strange discrepancies to you, but i quite like you and so i choose to ignore them until it's all horribly wrong and i float off to find love somewhere else.

i'm twenty five and i'm a fucking mess. you seem to like my mess. i dress up to suit you, i sleep in a dirty bed full of holes in the sheets. you think it's cool not to change your bedclothes and stay filthy. it's rock and roll baby. i squirm with the dirt, get up, go home and scrub myself clean. i smile at you. you smile at me but you're already looking at some other goth girl who doesn't mind the dirt.

i'm twenty six, a photographer and artist now. you charm me into your life with music and creativity. i let you in but you're a boy…a fucking boy! you wreck my friendships and jeopardise everything and i tire of it. you hold on tightly. you fuck me so fast i could almost think you hadn't started yet. i'm sick of not getting my own satisfaction now and it's really starting to piss me off. we call it a day. thank god. i leave you with your guitar and your charm. you leave me with a bit of peace. does anyone understand what you were really like under your loveable exterior? tiring…but i did love you too.

i'm twenty nine. your political perspectives intrigue me and excite me. your calmness appeals to me after all of the others….but there's nothing coming back beyond obedience and a predictable hum of mundane day-to-day observations. oh dear. i'm pregnant! but it's all okay cos you're a decent bloke.

i'm thirty two and you are really challenging me. you excite me, you're my friend. i've got a baby and i'm quite a lot older than you. it doesn't matter? great! thirteen years later i've got three babies and a broken marriage. but we had some fun along the way. all went tits-up but the overwhelming human desire to be loved carried it along for years; more years than it probably should have lasted…and i loved you too.

i'm forty six now….random encounters, excruciating dates, some wild fun and some absolute fucking mayhem.

i will no longer compromise on my sex life, my emotional needs, my desires for honest, open communication, my integrity, my passions, my independence, my intuition, my truth. i will love you as i wish to be loved and you will love me back the same way or we won't bother. i will receive all i deserve or i will not engage. why would i when i could just play and have fun otherwise? the overwhelming human desire to be loved has stopped chasing rainbows and is looking at your beautiful form, pondering, acknowledging and recognising herself in you.

the overwhelming human desire to be loved is pointless without self-love or instinct and intuition are made liars and cheats. no more lies.

writer

the rain started to fall in heavy, fat, globulous, drops; the kind of rain that precedes a torrential downpour. it was hot and humid and the woman hadn't been able to get out for days now; this heat sunk her into some kind of catatonic inertia which had the effect of stopping time. in the three days that it had been over 35 degrees and wet with heavy, overbearing humidity, she had written loads though...absolutely loads. she'd not left the apartment for the whole time and was now reduced to eating the old, unopened packets of over-fancy biscuits and strange tinned vegetables that she couldn't name, which had been left in the kitchen cupboards when she got there. the place was a fucking mess...

her words had flowed from her though; not like the precise choreography of a smooth moving russian ballet, more like the stain that runs into a kid's trousers when he leaves the lid off the ink-pen and shoves it crudely into his pocket. it had been messy!

she'd let the words come; censoring nothing and a small beast had been born. it had run amok in the flat, smashing things up, things that didn't belong to her, but she had just continued with her writing as if it wasn't there...tap, tap, tapping on the keyboard, breaking only occasionally for more ice for her whisky when she tired of warm liquid in all that heat. the phone had rung incessantly, irritating her more than the constant high pitched buzz of the mosquitoes in the flat. she'd pulled out the connection in the end but of course the mosquitoes had continued to bite and the beast just slapped her all the harder in trying to stop them feeding on her blood. she felt raw and exposed. it was too fucking hot for clothes. cigarette packets strewn everywhere, she'd had two hundred of those thank god...duty free on the way in. ashtrays bulging, dirty plates on every surface, chaos...but beautiful words were dancing with her...a naked tango of exquisite peace.

she let her mind sink into the words. she felt herself falling. writing sustained her. writing was her dark lover. she would meet with him in the seedy corridors of beaten hotels. she would meet with him under broken streetlamps in deserted alleyways. she would devour him with a greed reserved for the malnourished and the mentally ill. he would seduce her violently, and she would cum over and over again with his fist up her cunt as it reached for her vocal chords inside of her, trying to rip them out as she shuddered into yet another sweet surrender. her demon lover recognised her innate desire for solitude and he gave it to her, in order to keep her his prisoner. he knew every part of her mind, every corner of it and every thought within it and she would scream out, begging him to leave her be, to allow her, her privacy sometimes, but he never did...he just kept fucking her because she wanted him to. and he was faithful to her! he was always there...never questioned her; knew her and loved her. it was that simple, that crude, that basic...

she wrote as the rain fell. the harder it fell, the more her words slowed, and then the chill of a breeze through the partially closed shutters. that was the moment when she stopped writing; when everything was restored to normal. she shivered...how strange. the sudden change stopped her in her tracks. her writing was done for this time....her lover left the apartment.

she tidied up the mess, switched on the shower and bundled all of the dirty ashtrays straight into the bin. buy new ones later…she thought, and she was done. her writing exorcised. her lover satiated for this time.

drug

she lit the drug on her foil and inhaled deeply. hidden in the bathroom, her bathroom, yet still hiding. the bitter smell soothed her; it was familiar, not overbearing, comforting, exciting. deadly. it was her ally...she loved it. she knew it like the back of her hand or the inside of her cunt, though both of those seemed alien to her lately.

she followed the sticky brown river of it as it ran down the foil.....hhhhhhhhhhhhh....inhaling deeply. breathing out. letting go. diving in. surrender.

eventually she'd had her fill. she waited a while, flushed the chain, arranged her clothes and her make-up, leaned closer into the mirror to check the size of her pupils. shit...dead give-away. applied a little more eye make-up and lowered her fringe over her eyes and left the bathroom noticing the strange, recently familiar smell of burnt almonds that seemed to be following her around....there it was again....

only briefly did she make eye contact with him, on her way out. pretty soon after that the night was about to get distinctly weird. the roads widened alongside her as she walked the short distance from the taxi to the hotel.

the.

driver's.

voice.

had.

sounded.

strange.

slooooooooowwwww, haunting, out of place, jarring.

"no, no, it's fine here...i'll walk the last bit" she said, as she got out of the taxi.

hotel lobby was odd. everyone turned to look at the woman who had just walked in. residents dotted around the bar. late at night. the two men in the corner smiled slightly and she approached them.

"hello"

"hi. sit down...take a seat. drink?"

um....wine...or maybe whisky? no, "i'll have a small white wine please."

one gets up and goes for the drink. the atmosphere is too strange and she's no idea what's going on. flickers.

"i have to go...sorry..."

"bu....."

"sorry".

she leaves, pushing the heavy red upholstered chair to one side and making her way out of there fast. where to go? faces loomed in and out of her awareness. people passing...keep walking. click, click, click...her heels on the rain soaked street. the light over there flickering like the people had. all connected. all out to get her.

stumbles home.

where.

is.

home?

unlocks her door. bangs it shut and stands, back to the door, breathing deeply. feeling relief from the cold doorframe of her apartment. he's out somewhere. she staggers to the bathroom and tries to get into bed. thrashing sheets. a strong sense of not being alone...but she is....can't leave but somehow pulls on her clothes and does leave.

she goes to her friends. taxi...a to b. simple. voices greet her, her friends let her in and give her a bed in a cold bare room. she hears them talking about her through the thin walls of the bare room with only the put-you-up bed in the corner. sad old metal bed.

feels menace. leaves. she knows her friends will wonder where she went. another place now. that smell is there again. almonds.

finally to a flat she can rest in. a friend she momentarily trusts if trust is the right word. she doesn't trust anyone, but here is the safest bet right now. sleep comes in fits and starts and in her dream, she is fucked by some great monster of a creature and stands thrashing a carving knife around in somebody's kitchen. it's the kitchen in the house where she's sleeping. mustn't let him in. he smells of almonds. they follow her around. the other woman in the flat knows this smell now too because she gave her some. there is a smell of fear in the air. the knife she is waving makes her feel a bit safer.

morning arrives…fucking hell what a night! drags herself out into the dawn light and takes another taxi over to the basement flat in notting hill.

"ducie….look at this for me will you? there's something not right. almonds again as he lights it up. examines it, sniffs it.

"fucking hell babe…strychnine…some fuckers giving you strychnine….who you dealing with baby? get rid of this shit!"

she throws it down the sink and a million tiny screams follow the almonds down the plughole. she sees herself and how small she has become. tiny even. tiny. barely there. barely human. almost dead. sick.

she thanks her friend for saving her. lights up a different powder this time and finds peace in the place of anxiety. 'i'll battle that demon' she thinks, 'i know him well' and for the time being she is home. safe.

then everything becomes a house of cards and she is standing in the middle of it when it all collapses around her. the cards sting her face and thrash at her skin. she sees her friend die in the corner and wonders why she just slipped away like that. she sees another friend waving goodbye to her as she walks into the centre of the flying, falling cards and then turns her back on her, not before smiling softly and revealing all of her rotten drug-riddled teeth falling from her mouth. she was beautiful once. she is beautiful still only most can't see it now…they just see the ravages of time and circumstance when they look at her,

"but that woman saved me," she says out loud.

menswear

men's fitting room, kendals department store; english equivalent of macy's or some other brand-known reputable store. saturday afternoon. sunshine. girls. clothes. all satin and silk, nylon and lace....you were a gonner really, right from the 'go'.

we browse and touch; look (furtive glances) and smile. short, knowing smiles that communicate a volume of words and thoughts in one brief moment. i want you. you turn me on. i make you hard. quickly. i like that. men are so outside in and women are so inside out. we've already done the women's department which is guaranteed to make you horny. all those pretty girls in their pretty clothes. all that leg and those rustling underskirts. panties...the thought of panties...i watch you getting more and more turned on and think of you fucking one of those girls whilst i watch you...studying your style, your moves, your desire. i need to see it so that when i fuck you later this week, you will recognise the man in me.

we go down a floor or two to menswear.

"sir, i'm afraid you can't try that there. it's not a fitting room and the cameras will alert security. you must use the designated fitting rooms sir."

"what the f...." (but we go to the one she points out)

i sit outside and kick off a shoe. my feet ache; i hold my other shoe on the end of my toes and arch my foot to stretch somehow. you call me...

"sweetie...what d'you think of this one?"

you open the door and turn around one full circle to show me. i say "yeah but maybe a bit tight. show me the other"...and you leave the door ajar, just a fraction.

i come in and close it behind me. "baby..." (i stroke your cock through the fabric of your trousers) "...that one looks good."

i unzip your pants and put my hand around your cock. we're in the men's fitting room. the voice of the sales assistant (male; middle aged) is just audible close by. you grab my cunt and tighten your grip and i throw back my neck and moan slightly. you shove a finger up my pussy and my legs go all jelly for a second or two. then your fingers (two or maybe three now) are working me and i'm all cream and honey in the corner. you can see me in the men's room mirror. i can feel you up my cunt. i drop to my knees 'cos you beckon me, challenge me...you think i won't do it. i suck your cock whilst you watch me in the mirror. you can see the back of my head and my pretty dress whilst i work you in the menswear section fitting room cubicle.

"that bitch should've let you try the shirt on where you were" i say, "security would've had no problems then!"

i pull up my dress, re-adjust my panties and zip up your pants...

"you ready baby? that shirt looks good on you honey..."

and we leave all of the clothes and exit for the car park.

snake

she sat in the corner of the darkened room licking her tail. the rattle was her pride and joy...warning, warning, warning! she hissed, no hisssssssssssssssssed a 'stand fucking well back now motherfucker!' at the approaching humanoid and carried on licking, licking, licking, preening....pussies! motherfucking pussies, all of them.

the light was fading fast as night drew in; she loved this time of day almost more than she loved the wolfing hours of dawn. twilight....half light...shadow-land....unformed mysteries approaching, the killing moon...

she was mean tonight; all bitey, scratchy, hissy-mean which probably meant she was due to shed another skin. she couldn't keep up these days; the fucking skins were littered all over london and were making someone a fat income no doubt but what the hell did she care as long as the damned things were gone. when she shed, she was at her most vulnerable, temporarily blinded, temporarily weak, temporarily static, unable to strike...senses dulled, bite all the more vicious should it find its victim. when shedding, a snake cannot be interfered with as all of its instinctive nature will automatically kick-in to protect the incarnate form. she was queen of the fucking night right now and here she was shedding another damn skin. they were falling away like the peeling skin on a bad case of sunburn...what would the humanoids know of such things? well protected to the end....every angle covered, they anaesthetised everything. fear...climate of fear. underground, the rebels had gathered in resistance. she lived amongst the snake people, falcon, lizard, coyote, jackal, wolf, ant, spider, rat, and even some of the big cats....all gathered here at night in poetic resistance to those who never shape-shifted nor even dreamt of doing so.

fuck it! she slid into a corner of her lair and licked and teased her skin into the beginnings of its challenging release. she mourned its departure, for every rebirth saw her different somehow and she was as tired of change as she was ready for it. she was just about ready to surrender to the shedding when she heard a rustle across the room. looking up she saw him approaching, he'd taken the form of a mongoose this evening so it was quite obvious what *he* had in mind! once engaged in a process second to their nature, the form could not be altered and the bastard had her again; she would have to seduce him or she was dead.

she summoned the illusion spell; a shadowy pall fell across the room as it began to weave its way into the matrix. she rose and stood tall...fucking hell! a stripper! who the hell made these damn charms nowadays? whoever it was had no shortage of a sense of humour that's for sure! 'aaahhh well, may as well work it' she thought, and snake-like she began to grind in front of him.

he was lost in a moment, two at most, watching her hips sway, her pussy grinding suggestively toward his face. she raised her arms (oh what joy to experience the pleasure of limbs after so many years as a belly-on-the-earth baby) and twisted her torso to the imaginary music. he was spell-bound...which was the whole point.

just at the moment when all of his movement froze, somewhere close to the moment when she removed her tacky g-string, she struck. she straddled him and sat down hard in his lap, destroying him in the instant the fangs in her cunt found their mark.

"now....fucking let me out of this ridiculous outfit so i can get on with shedding this damn skin" she spat, transformed once again to snake.

the mongoose lay whimpering, happy, spent.

snake queen loved him really.

shedding

she lay squirming on the floor beside the skin she had just shed. she didn't recognise herself in this new form yet. it was a different skin; somehow connected to very ancient dna codes that stirred something in her that had slept for a long, long time. it was tight this skin. it was uncomfortable. it had a tendency to break into song at the drop of a hat which pissed her off immensely. it was all julie andrews. snake and julie andrews was a hard one to call. fortunately, she had become adept at adjusting very rapidly to the new skins, and as a result, she was able to simply look upon this one (with a little scorn) and accept it.

"god is a fuckin' warm blooded creature...i always knew it" she hissed. "bastard!"

she couldn't stop weeping and the water was freakin' her out...snakes don't like water as a rule (only those sly water serpents that none of the land-bounds liked anyway....can't trust a belly-on-the-earth that does the water element you know). cry cry cry...the water was freakin' her out and didn't look like stopping. fucking raindrops on roses and whiskers on kittens...i eat kittens as a rule, she thought.... hissssssss..... hissssssss...... love was making a shoe of her, or a handbag perhaps, but not a coiled serpent ready to bite, that's for sure.

was it time to metamorphose before it was too late? falcon was circling overhead....waiting for flight, screeching for freedom....eye on the prey. snake was normally so good at this...was she becoming too earth-bound? no, her skin was simply having trouble re-adjusting. it kept snagging on branches and there would be blood and guts spilling out behind her. if she wasn't careful the natural healers would be after drinking her blood and ingesting her entrails for their own benefit. longevity and libido grace of a serpents fire...she slithered into the corner and found a dark shadow that offered comfort. it was littered with the shed skins of other snakes.

"oh well" she thought, "at least i'm not alone"....

and she fixed a beady glass black eye on the cave entrance. waiting for the moment of sunrise when she would bask in the warmth. as long as there was desert and a cactus at hand, preferably an hallucinogen, she would be alright.

perhaps i'll take flight on falcon's wing tomorrow she thought, as she pondered julie andrews...

jesus was a hooker

jesus was a good guy apparently. misunderstood. consort of prostitutes and thieves. as it should be. no fear. jesus liked to hang out and give himself for a small fee, loaves and fishes usually, for which he was handsomely rewarded in adulation and no small amount of judgment. reverie and fear.

the prostitute.

we are all prostitutes. trading in one thing or another. selling what we've got. genital fixations creating more trouble than needs be and giving the law-makers something to justify their fees.

"can i wash your feet?" he asked me. "will you piss on my friend?" "would you stay overnight for three hundred?" jesus no! no kissing, no oral, no anal. don't do overnight. clear? jesus may have wanted to save you but that's your wife's job now sweetie....

jesus was a hooker and i'm elvis....you like my hip swinging thing baby?

the most exalted potentate of love

you arrive at my house looking all gorgeous, sexy, enticing.

you bring me things; take care of my sorry sick ass. you spent the night batting monster sized flies out of kid's dreams; i spent the night batting monster sized monsters out of reality.

you arrive unexpected. i have no make-up on, my hair is limp, my nose an angry red my skin all blotched with the signs of fever. i thrashed around last night knowing i was fighting the big fight....expelling, releasing, letting go, surrendering.

to love. to loving. to being loved.

you fucker! you turn me into barbie with a chainsaw. i turn you into ken in a dress.

you arrive and tell me..."by the way sweetie, if your delirium is about love, i'm going to make it worse for you...i love you!" and i am momentarily speechless. then i want to cry and howl. then i want to spit and scream. falcon circles, snake hisses, julie andrews starts fucking singing again. 'the hills are alive......' and i curl up under the duvet, just in time to hear you say "ok sweetie, don't make a big deal out of it."

god, you're such a bloke.

you bring me violet and rose flavoured chocolates and speak of dirty sex whilst i eat out the insides of the fondant creams. you bring me highbrow newspapers and sit pondering the headlines whilst i scour the magazine for the fashion pages; i'm that superficial. i drink potions of sage and rosemary and you mock me. "every illness has a mind/body/spirit connection baby" i say, and you say, "why don't you come and sit on my face sweetie". boy, girl. girl, boy.

you wear your clothes well, a certain look. you keep yourself tight, a certain restraint. you fear love as much as i do yet some fucker thought it would be fun to throw us together...see who runs first and furthest but i just get sick from my inability to run...and i want to hiss and howl whilst you pretend to piss and prowl. dog boy, cat girl.

we began over beer in a pub. it was that simple. i knew you were important even then.

you sent me texts and we met over bitter espressos and talked of erotic art. we found erich kroll and elmer batters and all manner of divine perverts. testing the reactions and finding none; felt exposed. we met again in a pub at night and some young man complimented you on your 'girlfriend's' eyes only we weren't then, boyfriend and girlfriend, though the urge to kiss you was a growing sickness in me. then you came round one night after football....chat chat chat. two-nil. fucking southern cunts! whisky, art, music, life....a tide of passion that could not be stemmed. you left at 5am and i was fucked all the next day...couldn't concentrate on my work and kept drifting into lingering pleasures of you and me.

you sent me youtube videos; i sent you youtube replies. our dialogue was entirely musical at this point....terry callier soothed me, curtis mayfield made you cry. jay dilla surprised me, poison ivy entranced you. msn took on psychic interludes as you wrote and i finished your sentences before you'd even finished forming them...and i was right. and you fucked with my head and i fucked with yours. i sent you endless texts to which you responded and you sent my mobile bills all sky-high-sweetie-pie. i soon discovered that our phone sex life was the best i'd ever had baby….ooooh, aaaahh…i'm gonna cum….virtually! i didn't mind paying a bit more for the 'extras'…

then when i wasn't going to see you for eleven whole days, you brought me (on my request) a t.shirt i made you wear constantly for 3 days until it stunk of your sweat, your aftershave; you. i slept with it and cried the odd tear into it; confused, angry, loving. the beginnings of a fortress breaking down. cunt!

in the middle of all of this, you ran, i ran. you returned; i left. i left; you returned. we told each other stories then hid from their endings. i knew you before, in another time. we'd hurt each other, i knew it. we had to learn to forgive and to love again. you started to approach me slowly-slowly like a blind man with a lame leg. i started to sniff you out like a panther deciding ally or prey? you began to speak in riddles that i couldn't be bothered to de-code. i began to let the riddles just be. you began to let me in and the more you let me in, the greater my desire to flee. the greater my desire to flee, the more i knew i was loving you. perverse bastard i am! fucking cunt you are!

does love swear at its counterpart? does love reflect back a demon alongside an angel? is love not all wild abandon and red roses? what of the ordinary days? what of the wilting dandelions and the cigarette butts in my flowerpots?

what of cold tea and sleepless nights and "i have to go (this is too much)"?

i'm falling in love with a man i didn't think would look like you or be like you or think like you…i'm falling in love with the person you are, not the person i want you to be or think you should be or would shape you to be.

you are tearing down my barriers and exposing the shed-skin snake goddess underneath. you do not fear her (though your heart may); i do not fear you (though my wounds weep with your expression).

falcon circles; screeching, singing, hunting, swooping, both captured and free at the same time.

i love you.

lick lick lick

lick lick lick...the old skin lay beside her on the floor of her bedroom. she had shed again and was left wondering, as always, what to do with the cast off skin. it had been a particularly stubborn one this time, all full of tight gripping patches that had clung for dear life and may as well have been about three years old yelling "mummy, mummy, mummy...heeeeeelp" for the way she'd held on to it. "you're....not.... fucking.... going.... anywhere..." she'd screeched, grasping the sides as the skin sloughed away. "noooooooo.... don't go......i love you" she'd pleaded, but skin being skin, snake being snake, the inevitable shedding was a done deed as soon as the process had kicked in really.

she'd been reading that day about how (insert american psychotherapy accent for full effect) 'process was the whole point of things'...not the goal, not the result, but the process. so here was where we learnt things? fuck that, she'd thought....just gimme my skins and get me outta here, but of course this had been followed by the usual surrender. oh sigh, sigh, sigh...she rolled her eyes in contemptuous acceptance. she was pissed (angry pissed not drunk pissed)...this skin felt as though it had been very close to her heart, her core; her snake essence. she didn't want to let it go....did but didn't...didn't   but   did....yadah   yadah yadah...shedding.....

so as it had fallen, she'd wept. she'd developed a fever of sorts, become delirious. shedding was almost always accompanied by some weird event but this one had been full-on and fast; hot, sweating, sickness that laid her out in her dark and gloomy corner, hissing wildly at those who approached. one or two could see her in these moments and dared risk an interventionist word or two. coyote howled, owl swooped; tricksters and shadow creatures who knew her language: permission granted.

under the surface lay bare a fleshy pale pink/cream, translucent form; muscle rather than skin, an exposed transparent centre of pulsing veins, capillaries and arteries coursing a cold blue blood though her being. there were about fifty tiny vulvas running along one side and one great big devouring cunt on the underside. every vulva had a clitoris, every clitoris a heart that beat to the rhythm of something like a tricky song (his early works). they pulsated in hungry four- four timing, waiting for their salvation. it (the skin) looked like a bleeding heart weeping a river of tears of salt black ice and lava hot molten steel; uncomfortable juxtapositions. it held something of everything of her salvation. this skin was not easy to shed…its transformed spirit was no easy ride.

"hey you…fuck you!" it yelled (it had no manners whatsoever and had yet to learn a bit of etiquette). "yes…you…d'you know what the fuck you're messing with here…do you…do you?" it demanded and her keeper hushed her as best she could. a fairly futile endeavour it has to be said, so she began to lick in the hope it would calm this new skin down…stop it being so fucking embarrassing for a start!

lick lick lick….the new skin was kind of bitter to the taste. it had undertones of a good single malt, with a high-note of lily or was it rose, a strange and heady combination. it was a deep blood red in colour, speckled with the beginnings of a dark, dark, indigo hue that promised to take over should she allow it. the indigo reminded her of that place she visited sometimes in her dreams…a river of souls in permanent orgasmic pre-birth joy. normally her new skins were tight and black; this one threatened to mess up all of her snake-like tendencies if she didn't get a handle on it fast.

it still hissed, in fact somehow the hissing was all the more pronounced as it fought against its very nature. "love makes worms of us all" it spat, unaccustomed as it was to snake-like idolatry and reverie. snake is usually feared; it recognised this and expecting it, had been surprised to find a lack of fear in the one who had triggered this shedding. he must be a hunter she thought cynically…he wants my skin for himself….to sell me or make fashion from me. he cannot possibly love my skins as i do, for their sheer beauty.

he came to visit her when her skin had just dropped and she was that revolting translucent pale cream/pink of an old man's skin. "i love you," he said and she tested out her rattle-tail to make sure it was still there, bared her venomous fangs to make sure they still dripped their poison, hissed to make sure her voice was in full form…

"hey thanks" she replied once she knew all were in working order, "i love you too."

shape shifting

the hyena curled its sorry ass back into that familiar hunch. it didn't know if it was hunter or prey. fucking hyenas...never take anything seriously....hunted...it was being hunted this time round. shape shifting into the hunter, it decided that today was as good a day as any for leopard. sleek, lithe, muscular beauty sniffing out the lame, the weak and the weary.

hyena stopped laughing and became elegant control. it sloped across the rock-face and took overview of the landscape below. the medicine of leopard/panther; embracing the unknown. three years ago it had come to her in a dream and sensed her out, witnessed her like a bone sheared of flesh and tossed aside; finished, only she wasn't. the vultures had underestimated her; her bones coursed with life. there was a beating pulse in there albeit faint.

languid, rapid as a poison dart through a bamboo blow-shooter, panther leapt and devoured her own shadow. she cried only briefly, a faint 'help' uttered in teeny tiny sounds of hopelessness and then panther spat her out again. gristle, muck and spit, flesh, blood and possibility.

she emerged as human. was this the correct version of the creationist myth? sensual, powerful beyond measure she liked her new form. she pulled out a mobile phone from the built-in pocket on the skin of her thigh and dialed a number she didn't even know she knew....

"listen, you cunt, i'm coming round," she began....

'the person you are calling knows you are waiting and doesn't give a fuck' she heard back.

growling and snarling, still panther in spirit, she leapt on a 93 bus and crossed town.

she arrived at his flat, banged on the door and then remembered she had a key. she let herself in. he was taking a bath.

"you fuckwit! that phone has been stalking me all fucking day! it's called me seven times already and taken me on a journey through automated hell...why do people use these bastard systems if there's only some cavernous black hole of a no-face-no-name-office working really fucking hard at ignoring everything on the other end? aaaarrrrgghhhhhh..." she howled, "and now yours baby...yours has gone all freaky on me too..."

"sweetie, calm down. get in the bath with me. come and sit on my face baby and let it all go" and before she knew it she was snake again and he was snake-charmer. god he was good at that....

the water rippled around her tired bones and soothed her weary spirit. he bit her neck and pulled hard on her nipple. she moaned. he kissed her and she began to melt...

she became eagle and slashed him to ribbons in the bath. the water ran all red and bloody and she became cat and licked it all up. when she had eaten all of him, she coughed up a fur-ball, spat him out and he was reborn her eager puppy.

she would eat only of the highest quality prey and he would surrender only to the highest calibre of huntress.

they made the perfect match.

voyeur

i dropped my laptop in a moment. a lost moment of dementia. you would have laughed and i would have said "what...is that funny or something?" if you had seen me. but you didn't.

i sniffed my panties before i dropped them into the laundry basket. inhaling deeply with a sexual curiousity about my own smell. you would have watched me and smiled if you had seen me. but you didn't.

i shaved my legs in the bath as my small son said "mummy, you're making the water all scummy" and i just rippled up the surface with my hands and said "there...gone now!" and carried on. you would have stared; considered the bits of hair in his bath water distasteful had you seen me. but you didn't.

i stumbled into the corner of the bed, slightly drunk even though i was alone. my heavy lidded eyes thought about love and i drank some more whisky to stem the tide of feeling and rubbed the bruise starting to form on my thigh. you would have watched and shaken your head, or maybe tutted loudly, or maybe understood, had you seen me. but you didn't.

i scratched your name into my notepaper and drew tiny little lovehearts around it pretending i was at school. then i scribbled it out with thick black lines and laughed at my own folly, turning to my list of 'things to do' and forgetting such rubbish. you would have taken your pen and written 'yes' next to my foolish words had you seen me. but you didn't.

i scraped off my make-up and pulled ugly grimaces at my own image in the mirror to see how bad i could look when tired and devoid of all cosmetic assistance. it wasn't a pretty sight, so i said "fuck it" out loud and went for a pee instead. you would have watched silently in the corner had you seen me. but you didn't.

i came to bed and looked longingly at my shoes. contemplated briefly which ones i might wear tomorrow. looked at the symbols of my life surrounding me. loved them. smiled. thought of you. you would have kissed me had you seen me. but you didn't.

exhibitionist seeks voyeur for travel, laughs and a future of dirty sex, longing and love. must be creative, have g.s.o.h and a love of other people's children.

love of whisky a bonus.

salome

salome looked down at the man at her feet. she leaned close into his ear and with the tiniest hint of her tongue brushing his cheek, she whispered....

"now dance motherfucker...dance!"

the man flushed and looked down at the floor to hide his discomfort. he desperately wanted to please her, she was his mistress, his salvation, his goddess of all things sensual in his world. he didn't like dancing at the best of times but now was obviously not going to be the time to present her with this fact. she stood tall above him, her long red nails menacingly stroking the newly shaved skin of his scalp. she made him nervous when she was in this kind of mood; unpredictable, erratic and sometimes cruel, she was clearly gunning for some specific kind of fulfillment here. could he meet her demands? more importantly, could he meet her needs? he looked down at the shining black patent leather of her new heels. she caught him...

"yeah baby, why don't you just do it...." as she presented her elegant shoe for him to lick.

"pussy whore!" she spat as he began licking.

she stood a while, observing him, carefully scrutinising his mood, subtly assessing his energy levels and his overall feeling. it was perfectly submissive, a little afraid with just a tiny hint of alpha-male resistance flickering in there somewhere. she liked that; her victories were made all the more exquisite for his attachment to being the dominant gender.

last night, when she had been fucking his father, his father had told her that his son suspected him of adultery. the younger man had been angry and had ranted at him, accusing him of all manner of things, mostly born of hearsay originating in the drunken gossip of the bored women and men who all too often found themselves sad and lonely in the city centre bars they frequented. he'd told him outright that if he discovered this rumour to be true, that he would reveal everything to his mother, including the identity of the adulteress. salome laughed to herself as she pondered his innocence whilst he knelt at her feet.

salome was a woman who liked to express her sexuality as she pleased; consenting and adult being the only pre-requisite for her pleasures. in the case of the man before her now, she could honestly admit that she felt a great deal of tenderness towards him, whereas his father was simply a great fuck. however, his ranting accusations about her (not knowing her true identity of course) as the wrecker of an already paper thin marriage, riled her no end. fidelity was such a fascinating concept....

"baby, you can stop licking now," and she moved across the room towards the stereo in the corner. swaying snakelike to an invisible tune already playing out in her imagination she thumbed through her cd case and found what she was looking for; a tricky album, the original and the best to her mind. she looked over her shoulder at the semi-naked man still focussing his gaze on the floor, 'good' she thought, 'at least he is relatively well trained now.'

she found the track she wanted and hit 'play.' the heavy, sultry opening chords of 'hell is round the corner' started to sing out from her stereo. the man flinched. she read his body language in a split second and capitalised rapidly upon his acute embarrassment.

"off you go baby...dance, why don't you," and she sat open legged in the heavy armchair in the corner of the room. the man begged...

"please mistress, don't make me do this."

"aaah, whadda matter...widdle baby not like to dance for his queen?" her tone mocking yet commanding at the same time. "just do it baby"......"no actually, wait right there, i'll be back in a second," and she vanished, returning some moments later throwing something in his direction.

"fetch baby....and then put them on."

panties. hers. and a short girly dress she occasionally liked to wear when feeling all soft and feminine, one aspect of her that *occasionally* found voice.

he slowly stepped into her things, his shame almost absolute.

"if i could offer you anything you desired in return for this dance, what would you ask of me baby?"

he looked up at her.

"marry me mistress."

"then make it the dance of your life you little fucker... make it the dance of your life..."

he began to lose himself in the dance. there was too much at stake here to hold on to his ego.

dancing, he wept as he lost all sense of himself in pursuit of his trophy.

grasshopper

the woman sat gazing blankly upon the creature she had just birthed. it confused her. women were supposed to give birth to forms that at least resembled their own basic genetic construct but this wriggling thing in front of her defied all logic or reason. the creature had emerged looking like some strange straw coloured amoeba with multiple 'limbs', a clear gelatinous sperm like head and the beginnings of a rudimentary personality. it had rapidly transformed into a grasshopper with a baby's head; some small relief that there was at least one part of it that resembled either her, or her human form at least?

she was mad as hell and looking for someone to pay. there was no way she was taking this one on alone. someone had impregnated her knowing that their own gene pool was contaminated, there could be no other explanation and she knew exactly who it was…..

claudia strutted across the path to the university canteen. she was gunning for some pay back here; her sensory stimulators were on full tilt as she sniffed him out. she spotted him in the queue for dinner standing next to a good looking japanese woman in a short white dress and high heeled tan sandals. typical! he was working his charm on her and she recognised it so well; she could smell the pheromones from here. she knew from her innate sensory programming that two things were going on here:

1). his cock was dribbling a clear pre-ejaculate fluid that meant he was eager and fully aroused by the woman beside him, and

2). the woman's panties were damp and she was equally aroused, though feigning only moderate interest on a purely professional basis right now. her smell told claudia that her interest went beyond the professional.

strangely, and somewhat reassuringly, there was a third smell she was picking up, a kind of burnt metallic odour that she recognised as the tiniest hint of fear. he was aware of claudia, though not because he could see her or knew she was there, but simply because he feared her, full stop. good…it would make her job so much easier…

claudia stepped back a little, she didn't want to be seen; this was too good to miss. he postured in ways she knew so intimately; looked the woman direct in the eye when speaking, responded well and with full engagement to her professional assessments of their work, smiled broadly intermittently (though not too often lest she think he was not taking her seriously) and his body language matched his desire to get to know her more. the bastard! claudia knew where her own strengths lay and she was letting this one play out in order that she could punish him appropriately later. she hung back and continued observing him.

closer now, he sat beside her at the table, eating heartily whilst the woman, conversely, picked at her food, shoving it restlessly around her plate; distracted. the man gathered momentum now, sensing he was in control. he was nodding vigorously in response to something she was saying and the woman flushed. over her shoulder the man was watching another woman in the queue; tight red sweater, knee length black skirt, red heels, the kind of look he found irresistible. the japanese woman turned to follow his gaze and in that moment, he lost her. she had seen the other woman and had she retracted her interest almost instinctively, wounded by the generic desire she clearly represented. she made her excuses and left. the man silently cursed his own carelessness and stood up to go and find a place outside where it was still possible to smoke.

claudia made her move....

"hi baby....fancy running into you here," as she looked him square in the eye.

he flinched; coloured as red as the woman he'd been sitting with ten minutes earlier and casually focused his attention on lighting his cigarette. he inhaled deeply.

claudia detected a new smell...the stink of sweet submission.

"busy?"

"no, not really princess....you?"

"well you know, here and there, this and that" she responded vaguely. "i have something i need you to see" she said, "come with me!"

unable to refuse her, he stood on the burning butt of his cigarette and ran to catch her up. claudia, already clear about where she was taking him and in no doubt whatsoever that he would follow her, was striding across the car park to a small dark outbuilding in a woody copse in the university grounds.

she opened the door and beckoned him inside. taking a moment to adjust his eyes to the dark, damp room, he looked at her quizzically....

"what is it baby? what do you want to show me?" he asked, trying to add just the right amount of charm in with his naturally submissive tendency whenever he was in her presence.

she turned on him, a cold vicious glare in her eyes. glinting, cruel? definitely enraged….

"you bastard!" she spat, "what the *fuck* is this?" as she pushed a small box toward him with her spike heel.

he gazed into the dirty card box to see it lined with an equally grubby frayed old blanket, on top of which lay some weird chirping creature with a grasshopper's body and the head of a human child.

"jesus claudia…sorry….i never realised…."

"no, well get this fuckwit…it's all yours. i'm not cut out to be a mother and certainly not to some hybrid freak of nature orchestrated by your perverted desire to fuck anything with a pulse. tell me…exactly when did you start fucking (insects)?"

"uh…."

"listen, don't bother right. not interested. why don't you just step over here to me and assume the position baby;" a demand rather than a question.

g. fell to his knees at her feet and bowed his head in natural deference to her superiority…

mary magdalena mackenzie

mary magdelena cursed her name out loud, followed by;

"jesus christ al-motherfucking-mighty!"

she was vulgar, angry - no...raging, and in pain. she yelled and then spat at the crowd gathering around her; tut-tut...such poor manners for a lady. if she hadn't learnt to tame them by now, she never would. she sighed....life could've been so much easier she thought. if only...if only i'd followed my mother's dreams, the expectations of my father, lived their unfulfilled lives out on their account, life may indeed have been easier...or just dull?

mary (nee mary magdelena mackenzie) lived on the outskirts of one of the toughest most notorious estates in central/south manchester. she grew up dancing to seventies sweet soul music until, at the age of eighteen, tired of her virginal name and overworked sweet identity, she ventured into the dark heart of the city and began to discover the bittersweet riffs of lovers rock in the nile club in moss side's after hours shabeens. mary loved the feeling of danger in the heavy marijuana laden dampness of the dark, edgy clubs. she loved to grind her hips to the deep bass dub of a song that sounded to her as if it had been written just for sex. as of yet, she was fairly unaccustomed to sex anyway which was probably why everything in this place seemed dangerous and exciting to her.

that's when she met him.

jesus (pronounced hay-seuss on account of his south-american origins), was mad, bad and truly dangerous to know (only she didn't know that then). dark olive skin;

he had a long, deep scar running across one eyelid and down his left cheek which gave him the appearance of a permanent air of sizing things up. this only added to his gangster kudos as no-one quite knew what to make of him at any given moment. he was unpredictable; a useful tool for gangsters and madmen.

mary smiled shyly in his direction; he nodded back languorously only she wasn't sure if it was at her or at someone standing behind her. the dj span a killer tune and the place began to rock in unison. the beers which were being illegally sold at a pound a tin, straight from the cash & carry plastic wrapping, were flying out now. the heat in the place was becoming unbearable as sweat dripped from the dancers to the rafters and back onto the bodies of the dancers again in some god-awful cycle of body fluid emissions. the smell of sweat mixed with the ganja made her retch but she didn't show it. she just stood there acting all cool. 'hay-suess' made her the central focus of her own attention, as in giving her some of *his* attention, she became acutely aware of every detail of her appearance, clothing, body movements…right down to the company she kept who were a little too green looking for this place but hey, she wouldn't have walked in alone.

hay-suess made his move; struck like a viper and now here she was on this damned cross seven years later. the bastard!

he'd had a thing for asphyxiation and oral sex (no consent necessary) and an even weirder thing for having his feet washed. his feet weren't even attractive and smelled so bad that he was prone to liberally dousing them in paco rabanne to mask the dreadful stink of them. the combined aftershave/sweaty feet stench repelled her but he was a moody fucker and she didn't dare refuse him his perverted and dark demands.

slowly, over time, he'd come to believe in his own mythology to the extent that he believed he was invincible, or so it seemed to her. he took more and more risks in his criminal activities became more and more vicious with mary and became less and less charming the more white powder she shoved up his nose. then, one day mary had simply cracked under the pressure and waiting until he slept in a deep, drug-induced comatose slumber, she had bound his hands and feet to the bed and began extracting her carefully orchestrated revenge.

first she bought out a rubber hood from a box beneath their bed that one of her friends had lent to her last week and pulled it roughly over his head. spittle dribbled from the corner of his mouth and he grunted, however, at this point in time he slept on. next she gathered her tools and arranged them carefully on a stainless steel tray she had bought especially for this occasion; six inch nails, a large mallet, some surgical wipes and a roll of barbed wire.

mary drove the first nail into his bound, outstretched palm. that's when he awoke. she'd never heard a noise quite like it. fortunately he was well bound and mary worked fast at hammering in the other three nails; one to the remaining palm and one to each foot. she crafted a crude crown of the barbed wire and shoved it down over his brow and then stood back and surveyed her handiwork. he was bleeding profusely.

then she left the room.

her own palms bled from shaping the wire and they hurt like hell. she cursed aloud and the crowd gathering nearby stared at her, shocked by her bloody hands and appearance and her angry demeanour.

"what the fuck are *you* lot looking at?" she spat, as she wiped her palms with the surgical cloth.

"think yourself lucky that fucker will never ask *your* daughters to wash his dirty stinking feet or keep them prisoner on a diet of dry bread and water. think yourself luck that *your* daughters will never have to pray for breath as he treats them like a dispensable fucking automaton. i saved you, you stupid ignorant bastards! *i* saved you and your daughters and probably your daughter's daughters. now fuck off and leave me alone and somebody get me a goddamn cigarette would you…"

mary was no longer the woman her parents named her.

she was exactly the woman she chose to be.

she inhaled deeply of her cigarette and recognised this moment as the moment in which she had finally grown up. mary magdalena mackenzie knows all the words to "i'm every woman" by chaka khan. she begins to sing them out loud now.

violet

violet lay on her back in the damp earth in the clearing beside the river. the soil smelled heavily musky, post rainfall. she lay there, staring straight ahead, which from this vantage point meant she was looking at the dark ominous clouds, moving swiftly, bringing with them threat of violence.

she clenched each of her outspread hands into a coarse set of claws and dug her bony fingers into the earth, angrily scratching into the surface of the clearing just beside her body. she glanced at the pattern it left. compelled, she dug her nails in further, repeatedly, until a criss-cross pattern of scarred earth encased her. she exhaled a deep and satisfied sigh. her work was beautiful. just like the marks on her body, it mirrored her anguish. her own upper arms, wrists, inner thighs and belly bore the same patterns, now as traces of white raised keloids from when she had learnt (unfortunately for her own aesthetic standards) that she did not heal too well from scars.

a tear fell from her deep green eyes and trickled lazily down her cheek. she let it run, echoing the flow of the river beside her. no~one understood her...no~one. everyone let her down in the end...everyone.

violet's sense of beauty was crushingly painful. it was both her blessing and her curse, but mostly it was her curse. it destroyed her. a child born in the wrong time. a victorian lady of pride and etiquette, trapped in a vulgar consumer generation that could only ever mock a strange and haunting woman dressed in long, deep coloured clothing, velvet coats, tumbling fire-red curls surrounding a coquettish face of immense soul.

her most recent encounter with love had left her dead inside, uncertain already about being incarnated in a human (so ugly) body, she wanted to take her leave. she was battling the urge to do so.

opening her bag, all covered in painstakingly stitched on ivy and the feathers of all manner of crows, ravens and birds of omen and portent, she took out a sharp razor, a small square of white muslin cloth and a bottle of some liquid that promised to clean up the bloody mess she was certain to make.

she sat upright and tore at the sleeve of her dress. her dirt embedded fingernails left a rough trail of wet earth etched along her forearm. she gazed blankly at the surface of the water and made the first incision.

normally, upon doing so, she would remain silent. this time, she let out a howl of the most dreadful, strangled nature and dropped towards the earth, pounding her fists into the wet leaves of the old beech at whose foot she sat. it was in that moment that she knew she could not leave; that she was beaten. a hollow victory.

angry, she began to prowl, ferocious, looking for an outlet. she had to have a new outlet. breaking the strong arm of one of the branches of the tree, she took her blade and honed the branch, working meticulously, beginning the work of purging herself as she worked. when she had finished she returned to her original place lying prone on the damp earth and lifted her petticoats. pulling her lace undergarments to one side she pushed the shaped branch into herself and began to weep in long, fat, dirt streaked tears as she worked herself to orgasm. shuddering as she came, she allowed her body to follow its natural gravitational pull towards the river and fell softly into the water.

as she stood bedraggled and sated, she took the razor from her pocket and let the river wash it away.

she mourned its passing as one might mourn a lost limb.

what's love got to do with it

the whore pulled on her skirt and tugged at the snarly old zipper in a vain attempt to gather herself together. she walked towards the ornate, gold embossed mirror and gazed in at her reflection, barely recognising the woman looking back at her. she dragged a bright red lipstick over her full lips and then laughed aloud, wiping it off on the back of her manicured hand as crudely as she had applied it. what was the fucking point....

she carried on staring at herself, opened a packet of cigarettes taken from her bag, flicked on her lighter and took a deep in-breath on the rough spanish tobacco. who had she become? an empty vessel it seemed to her. a tableau upon which any passing punter would leave his mark and then fuck off home again. wives and children skipping happily. whores and junkies staring back at themselves....a matrix of unfulfilled dreams and unmet longing. jesus! she couldn't even cum any more, deadened from years of practice; a hooker's mantra..."as long as i don't cum, i remain clean." she had so successfully told herself this over the years that a part of her had died.

and what of her heart....she didn't even recognise her own face: there was no chance of her recognising her own heart. it was a charred black hole of cynical desire and sweetheart dreams all mixed up together with acid teardrops.

she looked at the notes in her wallet, three brand new, crisp, lovely red fifties, two twenties and a ten and one less condom than she'd had an hour ago; she laughed. she pulled out the lipstick again, re-applied it professionally and shook herself off, metaphorically shaking off her opium-like trance as she did so.

"aah, fuck it!" she said aloud as she left the room, "tina turner got it right enough...what's love got to do with it?"

she pressed the elevator button for the ground floor, heels clicking on the marble hotel floor as she left via the revolving doors.

exit into the rain. another day, another dollar....

whisky

"bring me a whisky on your way back in would you baby." it was a command rather than a question.

claudia relaxed into the terrace chairs, large enough for lounging but austere enough not to accidentally fall asleep upon. she didn't want to sleep. dressed in black, she had only just discussed with her lover the symbolism of her wearing black these days...

"sweetie...don't you think my wardrobe has changed lately? it's all colours and frills now isn't it honey? these days, if i *wear* black it's a sure sign i'm in a 'black' sort of a mood...you know...edgy, tense, looking for something," and here she was dressed head to toe in black. her lover was guarded.

he returned with the whisky and placed it on the grubby surface of the glass table in front of her. the dirty streaks were pulling her awareness and bugging her. "fetch a cloth would you baby...i don't like that," she gestured her head toward the marked surface. the man gritted his teeth and went to fetch a cloth...

"yes darling," he replied.

he returned with the cloth.

"clean it!" she said.

his eyes flickered fire.

she smirked. "ooh baby doesn't like that i see." she laughed at him and her mood turned....

"get on your knees - now!"

he dipped to his knees and began to scrub the surface. the streaks spread further across the table top like a greasy metaphor for her irritation. seeping, permeating, unmoving.

"give me the cloth why don't you baby and let someone who knows what they're doing sort it out." he fucked off out of there before he said something he would regret, only it was too late.

"where the fuck do you think you're going little doggy? come..." and she whistled. you could almost feel the hairs on the back of his neck bristle.

"darling, i couldn't help but notice that you had a fifty in your wallet earlier. go and fetch it and bring it to me...i have a little job for you."

he returned with the money. she was standing, tapping her long manicured nails on the ceiling to floor glass windows of the terrace.

"on your knees now!" she instructed.

he sighed deeply...when the fuck did she get to know him so well? he knelt. she moved closer. she leant forward and whispered in his ear...

"now then little boy, i have a task for you. first you pay me, then if you're really fucking lucky you get to eat my panties," and she lifted her skirt to show her natural tan tights, pink satin underclothes and the tiniest hint of her pubic hair. he looked to the floor in natural deference. his erection grew harder with her growing sense of power. it was then that she spat on him. he was shocked at first, but then disturbingly aroused.

"aaah, you like that don't you baby?" she had assessed in an instant the minute details of his body language; as she always did).

she pulled him closer. "eat!" she commanded, as his face grew redder with shame. he was paying for this?

claudia talked to him when they fucked. she reveled in words and created fantasies like he'd never heard spoken out loud or admitted before. she liberated him.

he could not imagine being with anyone else. he was addicted to her dark, creative imagination and her seemingly endless ability to expose more and more of his secrets.

she began talking about relationships..."baby, don't you think relationships are strange?" he was instantly on edge..."i mean, we set up all of these expectations and judgments but who the fuck knows what really goes on or what makes a really healthy relationship? i mean, you and me, we share all kinds of stuff don't we, but if anyone else knew the level of it, we'd be judged and even condemned in some circles." he was eating her pussy as instructed and hadn't stopped because he hadn't been told to stop yet. he knew her well.

"you know what i'm saying baby...get this...it really pisses me off that people get into these 'coupley' situations and then spend years destroying each other. why not just accept that to be in 'relationship' is a fucking mess and one of the biggest challenges we face, and then stop looking for ways out all the time? accept it as it is, as long as it's honest...a fucking contradictory mess!"

he was getting tired. was she going to stop philosophizing and focus on cumming, he wondered. she could take forever when she was in this sort of a mood. he went to muffle a reply. she stiffened. angry? hell yes...

she took off her panties and shoved them hard into his mouth, at which point he almost came. watching him, responding to him, she ran her nails over his scalp, grabbed at his hair and drove his tongue and face further into her.

then, just at the precise moment she came, in shuddering heavy movements that racked her whole body as if in some ritual release, he heard her hoarse whisper,

"i love you, you cunt!"

he could not imagine being with anyone else.

the barrenness of unfulfilled longing

there is a pain in my gut that i cannot describe. it eats away at me. it needs feeding regularly or else it threatens to subsume me. when it is fed, it rests a while but it always fucking returns, catching me out whenever it can. it makes me feel sad and scared. it is a bleak dark void-space of nothingness and nihilistic yearning.

i try to appease it at times, and at times i succeed. other times i just let it be, watch it from a distance (a cautious distance). it plays with dolls like a therapist might, positioning them for information. barbie gets a bit tricky sometimes which goes against her barbie nature and creates a tension evident in her taut plastic smile and her taut plastic snatch. ken just keeps on smiling, pearly white teeth laid out in neat rows of charm and alpha-male hormones. barbie's whore-moans make ken happy. the dolls explain things quite well. the yearning finds acceptance and a certain status quo. you come, i run, i come, you become...something or other. and then i float again in some orphic ocean of morphine dreams and fleeting remembering.

then the longing is back and the urge to destroy returns. the self or the other?

the longing threatens to engulf me. i take barbie and ken out and pretend to make them fuck. that doesn't work. i take them out and make a cosy home. that doesn't work. it's made of sweets and biscuits on one side and you eat it. it's made of pills and drink on the other side and i eat it. it collapses leaving more longing. barbie pulls on boxing gloves and makes ready to fight with her beloved. he doesn't want to fight; he wants to luurvve baby....

barbie and ken get thrown against the wall and the therapist gets out the rorschach pad instead. "what do you see here?" a hungry giant i reply. it's always fucking hungry. i begin to whistle in the boredom of her analysis. time to go.

the yearning is made no better for all of the dolls, the pills, the sweets and the time. the yearning just has to pass in its own time.

strong

you kept the thing secreted about your person at all times. its silent beating heart sustained you. it reassured you and in fact, there was some suspicion on my part that it kept you standing upright. kind of like a cellotape maze of unfathomable significance. one night, i realised this. i saw the thing and wept. you did not witness my tears. they fell silent on the inside of me.

this being, it had its own small ego which had such an enormous amount of control over you that you feared, if it left you, you would collapse. when i saw it, i too feared that you would not know how to exist without it.

it entered into every aspect of our relationship. it had a perverse tendency to announce itself in the middle of sex. almost inevitably at one moment or another i would realise that there were more than two of us in the bed. i grew weary of making room for it, but only when i recognised that i may have to. until that moment, it had lain dormant, waiting for its time. i had fully embraced our sex. i had celebrated our fucking with an unrivalled freedom. i had celebrated our physicality like nothing that had come before until that small being decided to show me its power over you. then, i looked it in the eye, and in a fleeting moment i knew that it had you; for the time being at least. would you survive without it? would it turn to dust and watch you fall alongside it if you tried to amputate it from your person? did it live in your physical being, your mental one or your spiritual, or was it, as i began to fear, all encompassing?

i was shocked the first moment i recognised your nakedness without it. i had thought until then, that you were attached but not dependent. were you dependent? did it define you this thing? did you worry that without it, you would cease to exist or to function? that's what i worried about after that pivotal moment. i could not find a way in from then. until then, i had mistaken the place i had in your life for a deep and intimate coupling and of course whilst i knew this to be true, i also realised, right there, right then, that there would perhaps always be three of us.

i did not underestimate the place in your life this little taped up creature held, but i knew that i could not compete with it. mostly, until then i had thought i could just let it be. then, in one tiny fleeting instant, i saw you stripped of everything; bare, vulnerable, fearful, guilty, lost, attached, held, perhaps stuck? i did not know how to confront this new realisation. it threatened to weaken me, to reduce me, to build up walls made of iron and thorns once again. i could feel them pushing to surround me once more. it was so familiar my fortress; i loved it and despised it in equal measure.

how can a whore compete with a holy ghost? how can a junkie vie for your love alongside a fallen angel? i don't know how to fight this one. my sword has become dull, its blade tarnished by a year or more of slowly unraveling my wounds and forgetting to polish my weapons whilst i was busy gazing into your deep brown eyes.

it has a remarkable strength this creature. its heartbeat has found a way to beat in rhythm with your own, offering it some kind of independent life whilst making yours a co-dependent one. it needs you, you need it.

it is strong…. perhaps even stronger than me?

snake ring

he bought her a silver ring in the shape of a coiled serpent. it was wrapped in delicate pink silk and lace and tied with a small flower, crafted of the palest pink stiffened satin. she opened it tentatively..."can i eat it?" she'd asked before she realised it was a ring. the wrapping reminded her of those wedding favours you get, you know, sugared almonds or chocolate covered coffee beans...that kind of thing. the ring fell out of the fabric, into her lap. from that moment, it assumed its identity. he had given her a snake, her symbol, her totem. she knew it was important.

he wrote her poetry on the back of old vinyl 45s. he gave her records, his symbols, his release, his meaning. the last one had been covered in love-heart sweets, written in bold red pen and was the most beautiful thing she'd seen in a long time.

he showed her his new clothes; always well cut, always finished with that something special that made them as unique as he was. she smiled at him. she recognised his love.

they bought an old book and began a joint quest with its purchase. there was a story waiting to be written here and she was twitching to get going with it. her heart was beating like some itchy and scratchy moment in a cheesecake cartoon. violent exaggeration of sentiment. divine excess of feeling. spilling her guts, bleeding heart and soul into form.

she pulled the tight grey t.shirt he'd bought her over her head and thought about him returning to work in the morning, a little sorry to be one step behind their routines because of her recovery. still...there was no rush;

this was only the beginning of their life together, she knew that now. fucking hell! it had better be a *big* house......

drifting in and out of their memories, she understood something beautiful about the meeting point of love and art. she looked around her, everything in her house bearing witness to that meeting, some things belonging to old places, people and times; ready to leave. she looked at the painting she'd bought so many years ago and saw him and her in its graphic imagery. she looked at the pop-art print on her bedroom wall and smiled: 'you haven't even seen my bad side yet' it declared. wrong....he had, and he loved her regardless.

she saw in him her destiny. she wondered how that would be. she felt it inevitable. she felt it. she felt.

her life was littered with him; his with her.

putting one tender foot in front of the other, she recognised the fragility of love. she wanted to wrap it in the pink satin that she'd taken off her ring. she wanted to etch it into the grooves of a 45rpm pressing. she wanted to create art with it, to embed it into something more permanent. she smiled and let it be.

poison

she dipped a tentative fingertip into the liquid in front of her. it was hot, thick, bitter and strong. he had given it to her on his way out. "there you go baby....enjoy" he'd said with a sarcastic sneer. shoulda been harmless but it fucking wasn't.

she stood rigid, convinced herself he was watching her; he had that effect on her. she drank with some plastered on smile that was specially designed to please. 'if he sees me now, at least i'm smiling as i drink, then he'll be satisfied' she thought. she drank in spite of herself. logic, reason and self-respect? gone.

she was still standing on the same spot, cup in hand when she dropped to her knees, gashing her shin on the way down. a faint trickle of blood started to seep through her nylons. beautiful, she thought, just beautiful.....

her mind started to expand into something akin to a desert. vacant, hot, empty. a void space of nothingness. potential or death? am i dying she thought, but the thought was all twisted up like a bad rendition of a rachmaninov concerto. she put her hands to her ears and began to hum very loudly to drown out the silence.

her body had started to do that cellular thing it did whenever she was afraid or vulnerable. it was morphing in and out of perspective, all alice-in-wonderland only this was no wonderland, more like a living hell. surrender. she heard herself counsel 'surrender' and she let go.

she laughed an uncomfortably loud laugh and walked slowly towards the mirror. there was a fairground ride kicking into gear behind her. waltzers?

wind-up hurdy-gurdy music all out of chord accompanying her ride...your carriage awaits you princess.

lipstick...i must find my lipstick. red. she put it on badly, smeared it across her lip, staining her teeth. she smiled. beautiful.

stepping into the carriage, she felt the velocity flatten her face into ugly, twisted shapes. battered, bruised eyes, stitches and plasters, even staples running up the side of her head. transforming herself or being transformed. shape-shifting or losing herself? in control or being controlled? the carriage continued spinning before she realised it had taken off with the sheer force of the anti-gravitational pull being exerted upon it. it began to drop at a break-neck pace. she dipped her pen in the ink and began to write....scratching words around the carriage, desperately trying to make sense of her ride.

"slut. whore. bitch. queen. princess. baby. cold-hearted lifeless snake. goddess. angel. virgin. crone. madonna. artist. mother. lover. slave. mistress. mistress. mistress....."

she wiped the lipstick from her teeth and straightened her skirt.

"excuse me sir, but could you stop this fucking ride immediately please. i want to get off...now!"

someone heard her, heard her assertive tone and recognised it. acted upon it. she stood up, taller than she remembered.

"that bastard poisoned me," she exclaimed. "well, i'm going for the cunt now and he'd better be ready for me."

but in fact she had better things to do. there was a man waiting for her in north-eastern europe and she knew that it was an important meeting. "better look my

best then" she said, purging the poison with a self induced emission of bile and the toxic waste of a lifetime of false beliefs. "girl's gotta dress for an occasion like this," and she left the carriage to find her best heels and nylons. patent leather and woolfords.
    done.
    emptied.
    snake medicine.

nil by mouth

she sat picking off the bits of dried blood from around her eyes. there were other parts of her filled with tiny rivers of caked-on blood; she was anxious about tugging at those because there were numerous scars and wounds embedded within them that she had: a) no desire to rip open and: b) that made her feel sick to discover up close. she could not speak about herself. her face felt mask-like, frozen, in limbo. she smiled, through a full set of not yet finished teeth and sighed; would she ever be able to speak freely again? nil by mouth.

her bondage was complete. theft, prostitution, drugs, theft again, escape, capture, escape again. recovery. nil by mouth.

a slight woman of immense stature in other ways, she was strong, capable, determined. she allowed little to touch her and few of her friends really understood her. of those who did, her appreciation of them was enormous; unspoken though. nil by mouth. lately she was getting better and drip-feeding a small rivulet of recognition to both herself and to those she cared for but it wasn't easy. she drifted into remembering....

"if you're gonna be my woman, there's three things you need to know. first you never question me about anything i do. second, you never chat my business with anyone, under any circumstances, and third, you never answer or ask any questions about yourself, me or our life together. is that clear?"

she'd been puzzled..."yes" she'd responded in tiny words that meant nothing at the time. slowly, her ability to make the normal introductory small-talk required in most social situations diminished. "what do you do?"..."oh, this and that," she would reply vaguely. "where do you live?" "oh you know, here and there," she would say, terrified of revealing too much. eventually, tired of dull conversation, people stopped asking. nil by mouth.

she had come to imagine any question of a basic nature to be too private or too intrusive to be spoken aloud, even if she was only asking "so how long have you lived in london then?" and her ability to communicate was vanishing. now she sat here pondering the irony of turning herself inside out, at least that's how she felt in this precise moment, and once again losing herself and the power of speech.

the sign over her bed had read 'nil by mouth' and had been scrawled in broad marker pen on a rudimentary card, duplicated and taped to the door. she'd noticed it on her way down. blue gown fastened at the back, all jewellery removed, her own clothing and underwear removed and replaced with hospital issue. it reminded her of her brother's wedding where she had had been stripped of her personal identity in order to be re-shaped as the perfect bridesmaid.

"please don't henna your hair again before the wedding!" her brother had asked. "c doesn't like it, it clashes with the dresses and she's gone to a lot of trouble to co-ordinate this day."

perfume (calvin klein) sprayed delicately onto the wrists, nape of neck and decolletage of all three of us; pearls replacing silver. even the fucking underwear taken and swapped. barbie. "hello, nice to meet you...it's a pleasure, yes of course i'm proud, yes of course i'll be next." she ripped that fucking dress off not one second before she was allowed and jumped up and down on the hotel bed, screaming wildly. censored. nil by mouth.

rules everywhere. sod that for a game of soldiers. people don't take kindly to opinionated women. "ooh, i bet you're a handful"....yeah whatever.

she stared deep into the mirror she held and felt as if someone had taken her entire body and turned it inside out. the skin was facing inwards, all of her organs were hanging crudely on the outside of her; exposed, vulnerable. 'who. am. i?' she'd asked herself…'who the fuck am i?'

she was waiting to re-create herself and was presently in the cocoon phase of the metamorphosis. 'don't push it,' she counselled herself; 'just be.' don't speak too soon. nil by mouth. good advice. she would scribble it onto a piece of card and tape it to the back on her door again as a reminder, for the time being at least, until things made sense.

nil by mouth ii

there was a numb pain in her right buttock, descending down the length of her thigh. it pulled like a dead weight on her leg whenever she woke in the night, reminding her of the point of entry of the morphine injection, long since dissipated through her system.

there were sticky grey rings of tacky plaster strategically placed around her torso: one on the arch of her foot (saline drip), one on the rear upper shoulder (monitoring pad), two on the front of her chest (various pieces of medical equipment), and a pin prick bruise on the back of her hand from a secondary point of entry (general anaesthetic). her eyes were dry and stinging, her face numb and swollen, her body blocked up with all manner of chemical cocktails.

awake again.....awake again.....dancing in a strange rhythm, finding pace in a new beat. night time becomes her; writing is her lifeline. it's a dreamlike distant one but it works still...an old friend calling in the distance....."hellooooooooooo, hellooooooooooooo. why don't you answer me?"

no words emerge. nil by.........

she imagines herself tall, six foot maybe, and amazonian. in fact she is small and buzzing like a fly. self composed or de-composing? she's not sure which, when, why or how. opiate like visions flash before her imagination. 'ha! i'm so tall,' she reminds herself. tall women are taken seriously. short women have to fight that much harder. 'i'm at least a foot taller now and no-one messes with me. they can't see me though...i hover above the heads of everyone...i wonder what's wrong?'

she sighs. everything stings, burns or calls out to her begging attention. sleep is really not an option. drifting in and out. imagining a cocktail of body- removing drugs. one to make my head disappear, one to make my bones liquid, one to rest my nerves, one to fast-forward time. pink sweeties, blue sweeties, multi-coloured pretty things, all sweeny todd candy. you know, you go for something sweet like a haircut and come out with your throat cut. open wide and swallow dear....

she does.

she likes the release from pain. she loves the absorption into space and nothingness.

there's something important going on about lessons, the past and love. there's something important going on about unconditional love. she can't work it out. she has to go too far back. small; daddy loves you when you're quiet and clever and good. small; mummy loves you when you don't rock the boat too much because it's not a very sea worthy boat that the family set sail in. small; brother loves you when you're ordinary. bigger; lovers love you when you put out, shut up, make up and look good. lovers love you when you bring in the money. lovers love you when you enhance their own sense of themselves, a trophy. this lover loves you exactly as you are, naked, seen, in the raw, anything, everything. fuck! there's a big hole required to take that one in. she feels herself in that cell-like state again, only this time the cell is anchored somewhere. she has no idea where.

she fights against the hand that holds her; wrestles with the change. the drugs soothe her. she understands them. love terrifies her. she doesn't trust it.

she likes the bruise on her ass where the morphine injection entered her system. the memory comforts her.

she thinks: 'this is gonna be a long haul to the finish.'
sighs.
exit stage left.
prepare for scene ii

love

i pour the coffee into my retro china cup; it's black, strong, sharp, thick and reassuringly bitter. i huddle myself around the cup as if it were my umbilical cord, fetal attraction to the warmth and the comfort of that bitter liquid. in the absence of whisky (i'm 'taking a break'), it provides some kind of solace, it's true. i allow my thoughts to drift into you....i remember.....

i remember when you cut my pubic hair; you trimmed, shaped and regarded my pussy like it was a prize lawn you were tending in the hope of winning the prize for best amateur gardener or something. you concentrated hard, focused upon not cutting me lest i shove you away brutal and hard in my hurt. you spat on your razor for the final touches and i was alarmed to see that you intended to shave my hair with no more than your salivary dribbles. fuck! it worked though.

you left me with a neat, tiny triangle of well pruned hair. i admired it in the mirror.

"do you like it?" you said, to which i replied "i love it!" you exhaled deeply. you like it when i smile; you say my face lights up.

afterwards, we fucked on the sofa, you with mouthfuls of hair trimmings, spitting them out intermittently so you could carry on unimpeded. it was the most intimate thing i've shared in a long time.

one week later, i lie huddled, fetal, in our bed. i can't stop sobbing as i go further and further into my dark heart. you took me there just as i'd taken you into yours the previous night. i don't know how to get out...there's no-one to throw me a rope and i dream of heroin saving me. aborting my feelings. i let it be. i weep until i'm emptied. you provide the tissue for me to wipe the snot and crap from my nose and eyes. eventually i stand up and like an automaton, i dress and then go out. i seek out my places of power. the river comforts me. i go and sit there, photograph my feet on the huge rock i like to rest upon, gazing at the waterfall, looking out for water snakes. there's none today. i look in my bag and find my notebook...i write....my drug. it soothes me to write. i create a story that makes sense of things. by the time i leave that rock and that river, i can breathe again, feel again...i sigh....i love you but you kill me. you kill me but i love you.

how do i let myself be touched by love? how do i allow myself to feel without drowning in pain? i don't know yet, but with you i suspect i will learn.

extremes of love and human emotion. bathing in you. when you leave, i feel as if a limb has been amputated without my consent. my body thinks it's still there. i try to pick something up and drop it because my hand is gone. i stand and fall over because my leg is cut off at the knee. i eat and gag...my mouth has been stitched up in the night.

i dream of your children and mine piecing things together. i'm watching. i can't speak; they can't hear or see me. my daughter is trying to tell me something but i've no idea what the sounds she is making are for. the telephone rings and drags me abruptly out of sleep just as i was seeking the answers. i try to go back to sleep to discover what it was but all i get is the distant sound of rapid french in the street beside my window. it distracts me long enough that the dream is gone.

i miss you with a hollow sense of loss like i've not known for a long, long time.

i cup my hands around my coffee and savour the taste again. familiar, acrid, beautiful. i like things that make sense. they reassure me.

i love you.

licked

she coiled herself languidly around the fat pillows on the fashionably nouveau bed. it was a pristine bed. the man had just left the room. mistake? or perfect?

the bed demanded attention. ongoing. the woman liked to fuck on it. it was her mother's bed. there was something terribly wrong about fucking on your mother's bed "ooh baby...harder...ooh yes! fuck me like the slut i am baby...what was that mother?" mother didn't breed a slut, mother bred a good girl, however there was one small flaw in an otherwise meticulously orchestrated plan, that being that you could've cut the tension between her mother and her father with a fine switchblade knife, and the girl had become testy as a result; an 'edgy little fucker' as her boyfriend liked to call her.

tension breeds tension. sexless breeds sex. curiousity kills cats doesn't it, only this kitty enjoyed playing with her curiousity. it brought her here now, and after all, who could say there would have been better things to do with her days than fuck langorously on mother's bed? fuck in a post sunshine, skin all faint chlorine smelling from the pool, breath all honey from drifting in and out of chilled beers in the patio terraces of mediterranean bars. alive.

mother was asleep (may as well have been) in a self anaesthetised acceptance that 'this is how things are darling.' father was dead. mother's lover may as well have been sleeping too, selectively engaging and disengaging as his rigid moods suited him. shit! why do so many people settle for a lifetime of waking sleep she wondered. would they wake up in the moments before death, realising they'd wasted so much fucking life that the pain of their realisation would be bitter enough alone to see them into a prematurely sorrowful and helpless swamp of yearning? she kind of hoped not as personally she could not imagine living with such a huge well of pain; such a stinging, searing epiphany.

her curiosity hadn't always been so tempered though. no...it had walked a crooked path and she bore the scars of that walk like a soul tattoo. here was the boyfriend who fucked her over at fifteen by abandoning her at a party for a girl who would 'go all the way' and who let him put his fingers inside her fresh, young, unspoilt pussy. here was the naive young woman facing the sudden realisation that the man she had chosen was a psychopathic woman-hater of the most extreme kind. wits. careful now...skill number one is bred of it: the ability to read a situation like a psychic might read an old wedding ring. then here was the kiter, the desperate gonorrhea ridden hooker trying to find a way to stay away from home...anywhere but there...drug addicted whores need money... other people's bank accounts will do....yeah...soul tattoo is right baby... you doubt it do you honey? bring your sweet ass over here and let me make you weep then and let's see how black it can get in there....

but then again, love prevails doesn't it? and look what a bit of sunshine brings out...sex, wine and a greedy desire as big as a bulimic's secret feast.

i love you baby....fuck me now?

inevitable

"stretch me out like a rubber band, you got my life in the palm of your hand"...de de-de-de-de, de de de-de-de.......

the track filled her with a sense of inevitability. she knew beyond all doubt, her destiny. in fact, she'd known since the first moment she saw him.

he had something about him; an arrogance in his walk, a simmering confidence in his (opinionated) points of view, unafraid of his anger...how refreshing in a suburb full of men who had seemingly had their dicks removed for the inconvenience they caused.

he drank strong, dark, bitter coffees, like her. he wept unashamedly when watching big, muscle-bound men crying over the death of other men. he searched for sweet soul riffs and dropped them into her lap when she wasn't looking. he also scraped the diamond-hard casing off her heart and wasn't always kind when he had succeeded in exposing the core of her. but then, neither was she.

she was an ice-queen (she had been told on three or more tiresome occasions), despising of all things untrue to her. she was an artist, a lover and a whore. she was a mother, oh...and he was a father. when she first saw him...she saw her fate. she asked about him; it wasn't their time. she did not give up. she coiled herself under a dark stone and waited. rattlesnake.

he was a football boy. leary. more than the odd fight on the terraces of some away ground or other. stoning coaches. striding up the carriages of trains, adrenalin pumping. "looking for fucking bother mate?" yes actually.

they were manchester lovers through and through. edgy: survived the streets as kids, as junkies, as whores, as runaways, as punch-bag boys, as reds, as the innocent and the corrupted. kiting, searching, truanting, leaving, always returning. the leafy green suburbs of leeds couldn't hold them, the dirty grey industry of bradford couldn't hold them. manchester pulled them back, time and time and time again like a crippled siren singing off key. fucking hell mate, it even sang them back from france and dreams of war torn countries needing peacemakers.

her: manchester had ruined her once. girls linking arms in school. lesbians? must be. boys dancing in soul clubs; rafters, the gallery, moving their feet and hips to dreams of london lights and escape. they were the nice boys. the other boys hung quiet in dark corners, inhaling deep on private cigarettes. she wanted those boys.

him: manchester had abandoned him once. the boy, making dens beside railway tracks and jumping school for the matches. he'd had a heart full of dreams. unexpectedly his dreams had lain in tatters at his feet. broken. shattered. destroyed. breathe....breathe.....

they made sense of everything in manchester. as a city, she made a vicious and glorious mistress. she held them both, waiting for the moment when she would throw back her elegant neck and laugh like the devil. fling them together and mend some hearts. deep, deep, love and soul.

she loved him deeply. he loved her back.

inevitable.

gogo fatale

the woman was sitting, staring intently at the shining silver blade she held in her palm. she'd bought the knife several years ago because it struck her as beautiful at the time. she stared hard at it as if drowning in her own reflected image; she felt numb.

the blade glinted viciously. evil. sharp. alluring. it was too powerful for her to contain the desire to do harm with it. outwardly or inwardly was the only question. outwardly and she would pay societies debt. inwardly, she would pay her own, in scars and remembering...as usual.

she took a long slug on the bottle of red beside her, breathed deeply and then slowly and deliberately ran the blade up the inside of her forearm. not deep, but with a blade like this one, enough to instantly draw dancing, uneven drops of scarlet blood from the beautiful line that the silver dagger had etched into her flesh. recently, in her darker moments, she had taken the decision to create a conscious work of art on her own skin; at least the darkness would leave a beautiful legacy this time. scarification tattooing, marking her story, her feelings, her emotions, her life.

she loved the fact that she had to wait several weeks to see the final outcome of her art. before that, the scars would be too red and ugly; raised angry welts reminding her only of her pain and her isolation. when healed, they reminded her that she was a living work-in-progress; all passion and the legacy of her own depth of feeling.

"coulda just let me do ordinary for a while here you guys," she spat, gazing heavenward in some half drunken allusion to a higher power. "aaah, fuck it! where's my pills?" as she grappled inside her black leather bag, pinching her new wounds on the way in.

she stood up and stumbled. steadying herself on the table beside her she browsed her dvd collection for some of her favourite movie clips. that would work. stop her cutting herself up too badly. besides, she'd drunk too much now which always made it harder to heal the cuts; thinned the blood excessively and made a mess of her sheets, and she liked her new bedding.

pushing the vintage horror into the machine, she sat back and sighed deeply. as christopher lees flickering image began to form before her blurred eyes, she allowed herself to drift into fantasy. vampires had floated in spectral masse into her room. appreciative of her dark taste in decor, more than the usual number had arrived to feast upon her marble white flesh. seeing the feast already prepared, christopher summoned his women to allow them first bite. she sank into the soft-pile carpet and made herself available to them. the first woman bit as she felt herself falling further and further down into some tunnel of longing.

by the time christopher took her, she was already committed to a lifetime's willing service

if i'm gonna get lost, i may as well go this way she thought, as the blood drained from her elegant neck.

in the morning, the sunrise showing the dirt and dust in her small apartment, she stood up ready to face another day, considering herself purged. she put the dvd back in its case and the silver knife back into her bag and began working on the new painting she'd envisaged last night. she'd no idea where these ideas came from but they always seemed to capture some part of her soul.

always willing to go into the darkest heart of her pain, she always emerged renewed. a shape-shifting phoenix of blood and guts.

dirt

he treated me like dirt. he thought he was sooooo damn cool and sooooo damn fucking bloody cunting reasonable. he liked to see himself a certain way but that wasn't anything to do with how i saw him. funny that. when your picture of someone collides horribly with their own and creates a bloody roadkill in front of your eyes. usually happens in the bedroom, often slow-burning its way into your relationship and then exploding like a dose of the clap. you know you're putting yourself at risk but because you can't see the effects until it's too late, you take the fuck and moan like a bitch anyway. god you were good baby....ooooh, aaaah, of course i love you baby....

he treated me like dirt. he removed my friends one by one, picking them off with his uncommunicative ways (they didn't like him but i loved him so i let him get away with it) and his nasty, caustic comments. i turned round one day to speak to one of them and realised they'd all gone. well....there was one left but she had no friends anyway and just hung around us....i think she wanted him. had i known then when i know now, i'd have given him to her gift-wrapped with a bow, only that would be cruel.

he treated me like a dirt princess. picked out my clothes and dressed me up like a barbie doll. stripped of my identity i became plastic, open-mouthed, ever-willing barbie just like he wanted. that pissed him off.

he treated me like dirt. locked me away in dark rooms and came to me when he needed something, usually a fuck. i became smaller and smaller until i was just one cell, hanging on by a thread of me. the cell used to morph in and out of scale...one moment gigantic and weird, the next tiny and all but invisible. occasionally, lovers have since taken me there in darker moments, into that morphing cell state. usually i run fast as i can when that happens. sometimes i miss the call and get a bit fucking lost again...oh well....i've more skills these days to pull myself together again. piece by piece. superglued back together. patched up with gaffer tape and numbed with whisky.

he treated me like dirt. all but strangled me once and then pushed my head down to give him a b-j...the cunt! power. he was a short man. he had "issues" my therapist would have said, only she came too fucking late didn't she. let's have a hug ------- she would say, always using my full name (which i hated), and i'd feel myself enveloped in her revoltingly perfumed bosom, caressed by a stranger from whom i wanted no contact whatsoever, abused again by her unsolicited 'hugs' and sickeningly off- the-peg lines....

"you know you need to forgive before you can truly heal don't you dear?"

"you know your anger hurts you more than it hurts him don't you love?"

"you know you are loved, loving and loveable don't you sweetheart?"

fuck off! i'm not your sweetheart and i'm rather attached to my anger...it keeps me alive. it's kept me from going down many a time.

he treated me like dirt. hunted me. found me. threatened my life. but i was more cunning than him and i saw his achilles heel. i played my ace. i got away.

i've been washing off the dirt for years.

there's just a tiny patch left now, on my heel....my achilles heel.

bloody kisses

it was autumn; the season was changing fast.
the air was so cold.
you looked me in the eye and i may as well have ripped out my heart with my bare hands and offered it to you bloody and raw in that very moment.
we were pulled together by some silent force that compelled me towards you. kicking, biting and screaming all the way.
i dug my heels into the dust path and left trails of bleeding black venom whilst you held open your palm and then stroked my face.
an angel vying with a whore.
a madonna standing over a junkie.
i faced the image in front of me, glanced at you and a tear fell from my scarred eyes.
i felt five years old with a coat that was three sizes too big. everybody could see that i wasn't the same. i felt exposed; tough, misunderstood.
my knees were bloody too. i climbed as high as i could get on the climbing frame in that park and still, when unable to get higher, i cried out with the pain of longing and loss.
when i tried to sleep that night, there were monsters under my bed. one decided it would devour me leaving only a trace. a remnant. a crumb.
when i managed to find my way back, i was dressed in strange gaudy clothes that didn't belong to me. the skirt was so short i had to keep tugging on it to cover my knickers. the top so revealing that everyone stared, knowing...judging. heels as high as the empire state. call

me a victim and rescue me please. you will sleep and i will weep.

i stand on the corner under a cracked red bulb, flickering, your cards pasted all over the telephone box. a car draws up and i leave. for a moment i think i may have made a very expensive mistake. grandma tells me i almost did but i heard her so i guess my oversight was a break then?

now; a lover, a fighter, a little girl. a mistress, an artist, a thief. i want to steal from you, everything that you have, only you give it to me, so there is no question of theft.

sometimes i cannot contain my feelings. they are so overwhelming that a shipping container made of solid steel would not be able to contain them. you could take me anywhere. innocence lost. childhoods spent. days gone by.

days of love, loss and longing.

freak show

jelly legs. you smile at me. big sweet sugar smile.
you have sharpened your teeth beforehand.
claw fingers. you grasp at me and i evaporate before your eyes. i've been practicing that move for years.
suddenly i find my eyes are open, no eyelids. exposed.
you find your moment in my staring lidless eyes. i love you darling (sniff sniff).
i sink to my knees. you grow in stature. you spit venom at me with the sounds escaping your puckered lips. i dodge. i've been practicing that move for years.
i am legless. you don't drink. you are afraid of drugs. afraid of losing control. i stare at you. my gaze unnerves you.
jelly legs. green. acid green. emerald green. rage.
you brush the dandruff off your shoulders; the fluff off your sweater, the bits off the carpet. the marks off the work surfaces. the scars won't budge. time for the stain remover.
obsessed. you begin to stalk me. you want to be me. you want me to be you.
tattooed. i will never be able to do that.
freak show. carnival. you fire the missiles. i laugh. i've been practising that for years.
the laughter becomes manic. i am losing you. you can't see me. you're blind.
lined up you begin to take aim. you shoot me down one.two.three. i play dead. i give myself enough time to stitch my eyelids back on and adjust my vision. i make myself cobra and warn you to "back the fuck off!"

you recoil into your house of fraser/waitrose harmony. your lover takes your hand. he pets you before he assaults you. you leek a strange kind of colourless fluid which intrigues me for a moment. you catch me looking and quickly gather up your belongings and run in embarrassment.

you hide. you've been practising that move for years. freak show.

truth

"i," she uttered in some grandiose yet concise manner, "am going to tell you who i am. you," she spat in perhaps clearer instruction, "are going to listen."

there was this girl once right, she was all fire and attitude, small, wiry, alive, curious, confronting even at the age of three. well one day right, she took a beating for her brother, too cowardly to admit to his own shortcomings. she remembered that and marked it down in a small notebook she kept in her tatty old pocket. he (the brother) had immaculate pockets. you know something...he even measured them with a small, six inch plastic ruler to make sure they were turned down to precisely the same degree. he measured the fold-over on his knee-high socks in this manner too. his sister (me) stared at him in dumbfounded astonishment. then left.

older now she, the girl (you're following me right?) was weaving her way through life trying to see it as an exercise in conscious damage limitation, only sometimes you can only get so far with that. boys were snapping at her pretty little heels now and her daddy didn't like that, so he pushed and pushed against her (oooh aaaaahhh) until she cracked wide open and fucked right off. seventeen and on the streets with the gangrenous alcoholics with the big hearts and open doors (no boundaries you see...no fucking boundaries in drugs and liquor). still, there was a bed, a place to lay her head to make sense of things, to buy a little time.

she got a room in a house. the room contained six single beds. what the fuck was that all about? six beds in one room, all with lurid pink bri-nylon or polyester coverlets. quilted. waiting. and a ferocious german landlady who wanted to make sure that our "boyfriends aren't black are they?" and to be sure that we were not "that sort of girl are you?" took the room and made it for all of one month before the landlady's strange and interventionist ways drove her back out to look again.

eighteen with a bullet...yeah baby enters the underworld and just smiles sweetly as she flows this way and that into this thing and that. a bit lost, she does what she's gotta do and lies down for the queen on the back of a purple note or two. red notes came later. expensive hotels, expensive food, expensive tastes. hopped on a train, a famous train, michael palin would've been proud. still smiling she shoved powders up her nose and loss into her knickers whilst she accrued a bank balance worth bragging about yes? no, a debt to a dealer worth fleeing from.

come and get me...boo-yah! come and get me...come and get me....whimpering now because she is still playing hide-and-seek and someone forgot she was locked in the closet. they stopped looking. so she jumps out eventually and goes "ta-da!" waiting for her friends to go "oh, there you are! oh do come and join in the fun so-and-so..."

but they don't.

hollow legs and aching bones. stiff. running fast in her sleep. looking around and seeing only dazzling white light. the world presenting itself without an opiate curtain was too much to bear. but she was strong that little girl. very strong.

when she finally comes round, there was a small business empire waiting for her, only it didn't quite turn out like that. she left all that behind her in the toughest move of her goddamn life. she'd directed her longing into her burning creative dreams, ignoring some of them in favour of 'going straight.' the big dream (romance) was too giant a monster to battle on her own, so she lost. she lay down again and took one for the state. for other people's ideas of who they were. bursting out of her skin were small, no tiny, silver and black worms; niggle worms, not-right worms. they would sometimes eat into her and sometimes bust out of her. she would watch, listen and learn. beat me baby....i can take it. love me baby...i can fake it.

one, two, three lifetimes later, she surveyed all of whom she had been. mother, artist, virgin, whore, junkie, friend, but never child once more. she stood and gazed upon her territory, she took stock of it all and then smashed every last bit of it into fucking smithereens. she threw plates against the walls, dropped glass into the bath, flushed dirt down the toilet and showered away the ancient crusts of her unhealed scabs.

when she had finished, she looks up right, and there are a few of her closest, longest friends standing beside her. she nods at them; loves them deeply. there are more recent friends beside her too; she looks them in the eye, a challenge meeting a challenge. love in the making. she sees the shape of her tribe and she recognises in it one very important thing, that above all else she is loved and she loves. she stands in the centre of her own life and wonders which way she will turn next. there are several paths in front of her; the crooked, the un-mapped, the dangerous, the easy, the contained, the wild and overgrown, and those with measured hedges, tamed to perfection like her brother's socks.

she will not be taking that one.

"were you listening?" she says, "i, will *not* be taking that fucking one."

october dark moon

the woman stripped bare, naked, exposed, nothing but a blank canvas now. write on me baby.

she stood in the woods just to the left of the horse chestnut tree. bleeding leaves onto her skin. scratching bark onto her bones. she wanted to become zero, nothing, nada, rien, empty, just to be re-filled, in the faint and never-ending hope that the re-fill would prove better than the original.

teeth chattering in the cold, biting wind, damp frizzing up her carefully straightened hair. that pissed her off. fuck nature!

skin all goose bumps and chicken flesh. pink-white. loose. not as young as she once was but loving it all the same. this body. this polyamorous, sensual, sexual fucking body. bleeding again into love's tender traps. she cried out and the tattooist dug the needle in deeper, etching the words 'you came here to live; now serve me' into her pubic bone, just above her cunt. the words nestled alongside her previous tattoo and would soon become a story. her body; her whole body for the telling of it. simply that. her whole body for the telling of it.

her story. etched into her skin. burned already behind her eyes deep as the scars on her flesh. glittering blue-black words flickering in front of her telling it how it was/is, for all who care to read. the words become distorted in places. receding memories of one, two, three men fucking her, and one, two, three women judging her. harlot! jezebel! slut! beginning to wind their story down her thighs like the dribbling post-cum of a greedy fuck. watching the path of it etch its way down her leg, she smiled. knowing. understanding who she is.

wind whistling hard now. an owl swoops across her landscape. she recognises it. the past. rain pelting down now. a snake crosses her foot and she howls simultaneously as it bites into her pliable flesh. it has her. it is her. she knows its medicine and transforms once again, the poison into the medicine. makes her story grow. flashes a warning hiss in the general direction of the pretty animals of the forest. bambi. cocnkey sparrers. bunny rabbits and blue-tits.

her mother would not recognise this woman. she drives past and fails to stop. car doors locked tightly against the threat of hitch-hikers, free-loaders and whores.

her brother looks up for a moment and sees only vaporous form, which confuses him. he returns to his work. employment. career.

she is still naked in the woods. hurricane brewing and her lover approaches. he drops to his knees and weeps at her feet. his tears burn acid rivers into her skin. she glances at the patterns left but they have vanished. she devours him. it's the only way she can love him.

 loving him requires careful attention to the heart. the heart is deceitful above all things. she sighs. she loves him.

nothing matters beyond that.

release

i release you i release you i release you

the mantra burned into her heart as she spoke the words out loud. the sound the words made deafened her. she continued regardless.

blinded by the power of herself she stumbled into the dark clearing and removed her clothes, one by one, carefully folding each as she let them drop around her now naked form. she examined herself. with touch; with her hands. with sight; with her eyes. occasionally with smell; sniffing the underarms of her own discarded sweater, and then the crotch of her day-old panties. she found her own smell fascinating...intriguing. the essence of her personified in her day-to-day emissions. ordinary yet unique

she moved slowly at first, tracing a circular path around the rocks and stones in the clearing, beginning to gather pace as she focused her attention on the woman she was releasing. in that grew an image of the man she was liberating. she allowed her thoughts to drift to him. she could smell him even in his absence; trace the lines of his face, of his body, in her imagination. she knew every part of him; cuts, bruises, scars, moles, birthmarks, growths, density of hairs, which bits of him were shaved, which not.

her fears began to chatter inside her head; it was all necessary. it was all part of it. she created this as a ritual. fear is ones greatest teacher. she could smell fear. it smelt damp, like burned out fireworks. sulphurous. metallic. it spoke to her...in it were the fear of abandonment, loss, betrayal. in it were the fear of rigidity, formlessness and despair. she had to counter them all. she sat down in the mossy earth and began the task at hand, opening her bag and gathering various items from the forest around her.

as she did so she wept.

after about an hour, when her chattering teeth told her she needed to dress herself again, she lay a moment in the cold earth, rubbing herself into the wet autumn leaves, letting her tears fall freely. she opened her mouth and released a silent scream which beggared to be heard. it twisted into an ugly protracted consonant and pushed its way out. savage ritual.

she was not finished yet. she had some journey to complete however, it was important she dressed before the cold took her and made her remembering of this event become one that was based in sickness. she had all she needed from this place. her electric blue patent leather bag now filled with twigs, leaves, earth and feathers, remnants of this place. she stood back and turned toward her car. the place was so lonely at night....it reeked of solitude. she left that behind her.

on returning, she took a small golden key out of her bag and opened the door to her apartment. laying her treasures out on the table she began crafting a death mask of sorts. when she'd finished it, she held the clammy damp clay base at her face, touching her skin and allowed it to become her. she walked slowly to her turntable and took a record carefully out of its sleeve. "we're catching bullets in our teeth..." the words hooked her. she caught the bullet and removed the mask. it had taken a part of her with it. absorbed it.

i release you i release you i release you, she whispered.

i release you.

on speaking these words, she became herself.

beloved

there was something so fragile about the wings on that creature. one look. one solitary single sharp look and they were ripped off sometimes, causing immense pain for the person who'd looked too hard at the beautiful thing. the loss of those midnight blue, or turquoise or violet-black wings was a loss sustained by all of nature. it was too big to just stand by and not weep in wake of the tragedy. one could only yearn and crave with a hollow desire, the return of that beautiful thing.

there was something so suspicious about the wings on that creature. take your eye off it for one moment and the thing would be there, poised, ready to sting, so people had a tendency to rip off the wings before the sting could hit home. before the wound found its mark and left its acid barb in the flesh. the creature could never understand the desire that evidently surrounded it to do it harm. it just was. it just was...

there was something so delicate and perfect about the wings on that creature. so perfect that you knew you could crush it in an instant and rub the broken, stunningly coloured symmetry into your palm with the total power of one who is bigger than, greater than another. as if you could steal some of its beauty in destroying it somehow, though that never happened.

when i met him, i noticed that he had a pair of the most beautiful wings attached to his shoulder blades which more often than not he kept folded away, probably aware that others would try to crush, rip off or destroy them somehow. he had learnt the hard way. he had gained his wings in the most challenging way it is possible to get them; he'd suffered the greatest loss and survived. his wings were precious to him. because he kept them tightly locked away, bound to his body to protect them, they were uncomfortable, crushed into shapes that were aero-dynamically disastrous and the result was that he could not fly with them. these beautiful things became a junk shop curio, all dusty and forgotten. she saw this and tried to coax them into flight. sometimes she was brutal in her coaxing and the frailty of him became greater than all of his potential. she was trying to learn how to become more gentle with her coaxing. less cutting and less harsh and yet she was also the sum of her own experiences which sometimes made this hard for her.

when he met her, he was astonished to observe that under her dress there were faint traces of something he recognised without shadow of a doubt as being wings. he was breathless, concerned, disturbed by her presence. he had thought himself the last of them but meeting her, he was forced to accept that other winged creatures existed. her wings were broken and charred. they had been wounded once in a great fire that had swept through her home. it was arson she told him and she cried. her wings were not pretty and white any more, there were bits of feather hanging off that she was afraid to remove in case the burnt shafts loosened large chunks of what little of her original wing remained. she had noticed recently that there were tiny soft downy shoots beginning to form and she'd barely been able to contain her excitement. she needed flight to feel her joy. she had constructed for herself some synthetic wings that allowed her to remember what it was to fly, but without the innate connection to her physical form, the feeling was never quite true.

she admired his wings, she perhaps didn't tell him enough. she knew his wingspan would be great if he would trust in their beauty again. in their ability to fly. he admired hers for the new growth sitting alongside the charred history that were the roots of her wings, the foundations of her magnificence. he saw her magnificence and wept in the wake of it, for witnessing it, for being changed by it.

she was already changed by him. together they had held each other tight and promised not to damage their fragile wings. there was so much fear in releasing them, in letting them expand into all they once were and could be again. she needed to feel his presence. he needed to feel her love. they were making ready to fly and the discomfort of it was killing them. but it was pure, true and beautiful.

they looked each other in the eye, each knowing what they needed in order to hold, contain this vast expansion. their destiny was unfolding along with their wings and it was bound to hurt. but it was also bound to heal....

bomb

there was a bomb see...he left it in that corner over there and from a distance, slyly observed it, knowing he had made it, waiting for his moment and then knowing also, that he would detonate it in my face.

when it went off, it hit me full-on. it ripped off the front part of my face, my eyes mainly, and i could no longer see him. in real life, he had sat there communicating psychically with me, running a tape of "marry me's" over and over in his mind. in his mind, he thought i had heard them. i think i had heard them too because i cried, a loose cannon of a tear rolling agonisingly slowly down my cheek as i picked up on his silent sentiment. i was confused then. why are you suddenly become dumb? why do these words not leave your softly parted lips? why do your eyes convey great things and yet your real life person just could not let the feelings flow or the moment meet the thought.

i cried when my face was ripped off by that blast. i felt the utter desolation of one who has missed the boat they knew they were meant to catch, not knowing when the next would pass. i felt the utter desolation of the betrayal of words against truth and feeling. words, words, words. liars, beggars and cheats. thieving little fucking bastards! i hated them after that, only i didn't realise until about a week later that i despised them for robbing me of my dreams. fucking words, words, words. a literary talent for genius and destruction. where's the whisky baby?

so, you detonated the bomb and you robbed me of something precious because of my words. you looked upon my lover, my writing that is, and you said "actually baby, i love you but you wrote that and so i'm not sure you love me as much as i love you now..."

the word....the bastard love child of the story.

i stopped writing for a short while. i began to disappear. there was no rope to pull myself back. there was no expression of my world beyond a haunting sense of loss. i needed to write. i needed to love you too. you needed to understand my losses. i needed to understand your fear.

you begin to find a way to piece together the shattered parts of my face. i begin to admire them in the mirror. i begin to understand the depths of your fear. you and i gazed upon it and wondered how it got to be so fucking monstrous. you and i gazed upon my stupid, ridiculous metal-clad heart and laughed at it beating all by itself as if it needed nothing when in fact it desires love above all else...to know and understand how to love. a human being. a person who nevertheless detonates bombs in my face, but with whom, i have become myself more than my lousy words could ever describe. with whom i understand that when you love someone, you love all of them, including the vicious and the ugly, the desperate and the lame.

i love him. ironically, my words are testament to our story.

libya

stella is sitting on the plane to libya. the plane is coasting towards the runway and stella can't help but notice that the seat beside her is empty. he should have been sitting there. even though the doors shut half an hour ago and the plane is moving towards take off, up until now stella has managed to convince herself that he is going to get on. he should have been sitting there. then the moment hits her; the moment when she realises he isn't there. it hits her hard. she may even vomit. there is a bag tucked behind the table rest of the seat in front of you should you need to vomit. "even if you are a frequent flyer, please watch the cabin crew give safety instructions. it is in your own best interests." you may even need to vomit and it will be handy to be able to locate the bag.

she gets up fast. "i have to get off this plane" (she's yelling now and panicked, thrusting to the front). clare is nowhere to be seen which is odd as she was sitting with her only minutes ago chatting about this journey. stella shoves hard at any restraining arms

"i have to get off this fucking plane. now!"

the stewardess rolls her eyes heavenward and responds with a testy little "why?"

"just get me the fuck off this plane" says stella.

stella makes enough fuss that the plane, which is taking an inordinate amount of time and careering this way and that on the runway, halts for a second. all eyes on stella. clare shouts from the back,

"what the fuck are you doing stella?" angry tone in her voice.

"i'm getting off this fucking plane right now."

stella has a bad feeling about the flight. clare yells at her,

"stella, what the hell are you doing? for once in your life you have the chance to see this through and finish off the journey. you'll be a real woman. it will change you. sit the fuck down down!"

"it's not even my journey" stella replies...." what the hell do you know? just back off would you." clare is well pissed off now.

earlier that afternoon, stella had been standing beside him wrapped in his big brown overcoat. the other woman (she hadn't recognised her at first) had approached her and dug her hands into the pockets of stella's temporary coat. she'd grabbed a handful of what stella thought were tiny seeds in some little pouch and brutally tipped them out in front of her. in front of him.

stella had realised they were trinkets, silver and gold trinkets. they had belonged to someone else, someone important.

stella had gone "hey, you sick bitch. you heartless cow. how can you do that?" and the woman had replied "well, it depends on whether you think love is carrying that stuff all over the place or letting it go doesn't it?" and stared her straight in the eye, the cheeky fucking bitch! like stella didn't know about crap like that. like the other woman did.

the woman had walked off. stella watched her leave. then he went after her! stella was dumbfounded. her jaw dropped open.

'i won't be a minute" he'd said, and she saw him catch her up. so stella is standing there in his coat with the things scattered around her feet, his things, and a plane to catch. she's on the plane now, trying to get off, and he isn't. fuck knows what happened to the things. stella wasn't going to gather them up for love nor money.

stella manages to get off the plane amidst thoughts of terrorist attacks. amidst thoughts of dying for a cause that isn't even hers. the other passengers are pissed off with her. clare turns away from her, confused about the mixed messages she's getting. stella gets off and has never been so fucking glad to get off a plane.

the plane takes off and stella watches another version of her life unfold. the one where she stayed on the plane. the one where parhaps he got on beside her and they smiled at each other, the sighed and read the in-flight magazine to pass the time.

she's off. she grabs her suitcase and pulls it along roughly behind her. irritated, she stops and pulls off her ugg boots and replaces them with her more familiar heels. fuck that's better she thinks. standing tall she goes hunting. she spies him on the terrace of the cafe, sipping some odd drink.

i. was. on. that. fucking. plane. for. him. she thinks, rage burning.

then she sees her. the other woman. the one who had emptied her pockets. stella feels sick. she is disgusted. he would have let her go. on his journey. in his place. whilst he sat sipping teas in some posh london cafe. taking the easy route out.

stella catches his eye. she sees his fear. she looks at him, long and hard, then spits on the floor beside her, holding his eye all the time.

he knows.

stella leaves. the tears are flooding down her cheeks.

stella wakes up all covered in tiny beads of sweat, realising she was dreaming. she calls him,
"baby, i had the most horrible dream, you won't fucking belive it…"

eating stones

i picked up the rock from the side of the river and stared at it. it looked tasty; i ate it. i scratched up a handful of dirt and sniffed it, wiping the fallen debris off my cheekbone as i held it up to inhale the damp earth, considering rubbing the dank soil into my skin like some dark version of a facial scrub, my very own exfoliation au naturel. if it hurt me, all the better. the wet earth looked fascinating, intriguing even, so i ate it. it stuck to the roof of my mouth and made me gag, but i persevered and then managed, finally, to swallow every last bit of it. i went back to the stones and the rocks and picked out another, only this time, i was not so fortunate and i cracked my teeth on the hard surfaces, astonished that i'd thought i could even fucking eat them in the first place!

opium: state of dreams cracking open and stealing me away. smoke filled head full of longing, like an orgasm that never comes. agonising, painful and fucking rotten to the core. there are two men driving that dream taxi i take; i am puzzled for a moment, then tell them where i want to go. "um, sir" i say "there seems to be a bag on the seat that someone's left here." i scrutinise it more closely, "and it's ticking!" they know this. they want me to do exactly as they say or they will detonate it.

opium: taken there yet again (ta~da!) and held captive in some no-man's land of empty landscapes and fear. fear, fear, fear....yes, here i am bogey-man-baby, come and get me. eat me! but i drift in and out of fear, tooo shadowy to even present myself to be eaten. lost.

opium: i love him dearly you know. why does he push me back into these corners?

opium: are you trance, shield or captor? if it is to be my captor, well this time i'm stalking you baby. i will bring myself out of this dream and i will rise magnificent again. opium will not claim me, nor beat me, nor devour me. opium will release me.

i stare at my face in the mirror. it looks different again. freaking in and out of clarity and total annihilation, taking me on some roller-fucking-coaster fairground ride where the big clown's irritating fucking laughing face will haunt me in its tormenting glory. it never stops laughing.... ha ha ha ha hahahahahahahahaaaaaaaaaaa

i catch bullets in my teeth and eat stones for breakfast.

my teeth are almost all gold now

boy

the boy looked up towards his mother, who was standing beside him holding his hand. he was more clutching at hers. trying to pull away but at the same time desperate to stay. mother's kisses are too sloppy by far. mother usually finds that his kisses leave an imprint of silver trailed snot running down the side of her cheek, but that's okay, it's her boy. she adores him.

he looks up at her, quizzical, wondering, uncertain. he loves everything about her but he likes to tell her that daddy is his favourite because he recognises that brief flicker that betrays her when she tries to pretend that doesn't hurt. he is afraid she will leave again and so he tells her that daddy is his favourite. it protects him from loving her too much and losing her. he couldn't bear that. he's only small.

sometimes he likes to play target practice on her in the bath. he fires little high-speed jets of cold dirty water out of the bottom of his camouflage duck. the water could have been in there for weeks and sometimes it leaves the tiny hole, shooting out a grey stagnant stream of unpleasant appearance at her. she goes "hey you..." and complains and he just fires it again and again, at her belly button, her breasts, her face when he feels daring. these days he is beginning to say things like "i don't want a bath with you, it's not 'normal'" and she wonders where he gets that from. he's still only seven. but she knows that maybe there won't be many more of these moments.

he tells her great in-depth stories of huge significance about the football games he has watched and played. she loses track as she considers her lover, work, the things that need paying for, sorting out and doing, until he stops, waiting for a response and she says "gosh, your stories are so complex and i'm trying so hard to keep up; that sounds really exciting" and he continues. she sighs a silent sigh of relief that she wasn't exposed for not listening properly. she would hate him to think his tales weren't the most incredible things she's ever heard.

some days he comes down in the morning, hair all ruffled up, last night's cocoa around his mouth, all dressed and ready because he has a day he likes at school today. he looks at her, presenting himself. she says "oh my, you are clever aren't you" and he smiles. that's enough for him. he has on a dirty paint stained tracksuit top and mud spattered trousers. mother doesn't want him to go out in those in case people think she is sloppy and doesn't care but she knows that he loves that football hoodie and won't get it off him for anything, unless she can come up with a really good deal. at seven thirty in the morning, good deals are thin on the ground and she hasn't even had her coffee yet. she lets it pass. who cares. what does it matter.

this time is his. it is his childhood. it is his for remembering. she looks at him and recognises that she will do her very best to make this time matter. to make sure he recalls endless hours of curious fun and freedom. to make sure that he doesn't remember her shouting, harassed and tired. to make sure that his childhood counts for something fucking incredible.

she knows she didn't manage to do that with her daughter. her daughter had it rough. she didn't even think about it being her childhood back then. she was just busy trying to live life as best she could. she weeps for her daughter's losses.

she could create jekylls and hydes of monstrous proportions is she was not careful. that's some seriously big power to hold. she's not even sure she even asked for that.

she loves her children. and she knows enough to know that that's not always enough.

november

stella stood under the broken streetlamp as it flickered irritatingly above her. it cast a damp sorry glow hardly worth the promise of the security she hoped it would offer her in standing on that spot. she chewed her already worn down nails until her fingers stung and her skin bled a tiny tiny river of pink blood, the start of something bigger perhaps.

stella's clothes stank; she'd only been out an hour and she was pissed off with the situation here. one punter. bad personal hygiene. no jonny or no money and with a stink that bad, odds weren't good. stella steeled herself for the outcome in the knowledge that her sacrifice would pay her bill tomorrow. her kid needed that bill paying. she needed that bill paying or they'd both fucking freeze. stink and no condom it is then.

stella retched as the john lurched towards her. he tugged greedily at her skirt and grabbed at her stained underclothes without any apparent concern for her well-being. he ripped her tights. fuck! bare legs for the rest of the night then and in this bloody cold too...shit.....stella was considering this as he pushed his semi-limp cock into her and began to pump away at her with as much finesse as a badly organised soccer team. all over the bloody show....limp was never a good sign, always took them so much longer. stella could have wept for her tiny self, the her that felt every grim moment of this stinking stranger inside her. but she'd grown hard enough on the outside now to manage that kind of foul and destructive emotional leaking. stella knew how to shut up and take herself somewhere else, in her still living imagination. thank god for small mercies.

some days, the rage she felt almost turned her into some maniac murderess. i could you know....oh i so could, she thought on the third or fourth punter of the night. then some nice enough guy with a terrible self consciousness and no chance at lovers in real life would save her from a killing. no love, of course i don't mind that you came so quick. and she would pull up her knickers and smile, waving 'byeeeee' as she ran back to the lamp-post on that corner again.

sighed.

huddled chicken flesh bare legs against the cold november winds.

took another two and then called a taxi to take her back to that tiny fucking mess of a flat she rented to wash the smell of all those men out of her body and soul. kissed her sleeping boy and ruffled his hair, just carefully enough not to wake him.

paid the bill in the morning, for his smile.

carving angels

1. carving angels

i had this dream last night and in it, you were sitting (elegant as always) beside the river. you always seem to appear next to water in my dreams. you had this 'pet,' a kind of familiar that you'd constructed from the bones and dismembered decaying parts of other ancient pets. it had become this kind of pink winged, cream bellied flying duck. i asked you why it had such a strangely calm face. you told me it was the skeletal head of your previous cat. that explains it then.

i sat with you for a while, wholly engaged in simply being in your presence. you looked beautiful. you've always been beautiful but you struggle so much to stay in this world and this world crucifies you and betrays you almost constantly. you stand, brush down your petticoats and skirts, gently push away a loose strand of your fire-red hair that has fallen across your emerald green eyes, and you smile a coquettish smile. you will weep in a moment, perhaps even howl for your pain. it sits ever-present behind your beauty.

i talk with you about the poison darts that lie scattered all around our sacred circle. we scratched the shape (the sacred circle) crudely into the surrounding earth and then sat, content that we were, for a moment or two at least, relatively safe here. we turn our attention to the darts, tiny little darts with barbed shafts that embed themselves in the flash of a second into our hearts and make us bleed, bleed, bleed our souls into a dark and foreign place we call home. few can understand that place though many will understand the isolation we encounter there.

when i leave i have to cross a ravine on a backwards ladder that i cannot fathom for the life of me. someone laughs a cruel laugh and so i grab that ladder and fucking climb it in raging defiance of their ignorance. when i am safely transported to the other side, i have to return to a house i locked up and left long ago. it stinks of damp decay. someone has been in a cleaned some of it up and i have no interest in who that may be. i can't remember what i came here for and i leave. i slam the door shut and shout "good fucking riddance baby" and go searching for a book, until i remember it's a book i have to write before it can be read.

elizabeth sees my scars and carries her own which look much the same as mine. she wears many of hers tattooed permanently accross her arms, thighs and her belly. i saw them once and they made me cry. i didn't let her see me crying. she would have fled in an instant had she seen me.

elizabeth and i will speak in tongues. we weave silver threads of luminous beauty, each of us holding tight to one end in the ongoing offering of prayer. ritual saves us. art saves us.

we carve angels into your eyes whilst keeping our heads above the floodwaters.

2. carving the dark hearted angel

when elizabeth decides she is ready to leave, i turn and she is gone, without discussion or consent or agreement. there was no ending, she just leaves. she really pisses me off how she does that because in all the time i've known her, i still never see it coming; her departure.

she's flighty like that.

she is so beautiful though that you would forgive her anything. she cannot sin. she cannot ever be judged because she just is who she is and we love her for that so how can we judge her. she hates that we love her for that because it pains her to be in this body in this life. this knowing makes her want to spit and fucking curse us all. i know because i see right through her skin. it is transparent to me because it is my skin. if she hadn't been the first to leave, i'd have gone just as quickly but i'm a sucker for her beauty and she just is, therefore she always gets to leave first. damn her! i want to be a courageous as she is. i want to just be. instead, i am far more earthbound in my sensibilities.

elizabeth weeps crystal tears upon porcelain cheekbones. elizabeth buys ivory carvings and old tin cans from black finger-nailed vendors at car boot sales on the fringes of suburbia. she hunts and hunts and hunts for tiny treasures that she hopes will offer her some temporary peace. i on the other hand, hunt and hunt and hunt for some temporary peace that will bring me treasures. we've always been a bit star-crossed like that. once, elizabeth wrote me a poem that i treasured so much i placed in in a delicate gilt frame. her familiar spidery writing, doubtless written in real blue-black ink, spewed words of such immense magnitude that i knew she had seen me, borne witness to my soul somehow. no-one had ever done that before.

once, we made a ceremony elizabeth and me. i was dressed in a black shroud and she stood beside me. i read my words out loud next to a wizened old hawthorn tree and then stood before elizabeth and the gods, totally naked. she then clothed me in a white shimmering fabric and promised to make me a pair of her wings from that material. she never made them. i still wonder whether they would have made me fly.

sometimes, when i'm really out there, on my island, the one we all know, the place we call home, i think of her, and i think of those who orbit my heart and i drop to my knees, wondering how i'll make it to be ninety seven, like my grandmother. i wonder how the fuck i'll do it. the next moment i am strong and clear again and ninety seven seems like something effortless that only life could cheat of meeting.

elizabeth dances with me in a circle of chaos and her screams pierce my spirit. when i am snake she is before me all feline and sleek, though very dangerous. when i am goddess of fire, she is beside me all goddess of the bleeding soul of love.

we will speak shortly about those poison arrows, her and me, and we will hold each other tightly. i will inhale her patchouli musk smell and i will be sure not to perfume myself lest it confuse her.

3. the game

shards of glass lay around our feet. whichever way we turn we cannot avoid or escape them and so we are condemned to walk across them to return. i start the walk as i am braver than her though the cutting of lass upon skin is more familiar to her. she watches me, staring, curious and somewhat envious.

i decide that this may as well be worth it and so i make it a ritual of unfathomable depth. with each step, i utter a word, just one word, though a very carefully orchestrated one at that. with my first step, i speak (in a level and monotone voice) the word love, and she (as i had hoped and imagined) responds.

she steps onto the glass and speaks. her voice contains the delicate tipped angle of her head and the fragility of her features. it also contains all of the agonies of her heart. she says murder, and i momentarily recoil, still concealing any trace of a reaction from her gaze, lest she decides to stop playing.

my foot hurts already. this is going to be a painful experience. i turn and look her in the eye. i flash my indigo blue at her emerald green and reply yearning and she drops to her knees. i want to help her up but it's not in the rules. i must witness...and wait....

slowly, she begins to rise. she looks at me as if she hates, loathes and despises me for that last round. she sighs deeply. she coughs, and then shouts really really fucking loud, the word murderer. jesus she's good. i'm not sure i can do this. she is an amazonian queen of immense stature. i am momentarily a fly about to meet its death. but then i remember the game and i dig deep into my heart and find the word that wants to be spoken. the word is jealous.

she begins to cry, though it is only a tear that escapes her eye. it takes with it no trace of mess, as mine would in their mascara'd garishness. she lets the tear fall and replies in rapid breathy stuttering near-silence, bitch.

then it is my turn to cry in the hollow emptiness of that word uttered from her lips. i keep moving, i reply quickly now. saviour. and she approaches. she is close now, i can smell her violet scented breath. she goes disappointment and i retch in the feeling of it. it is too much, but i have a job to do here. i say fake and she finds her fire now. she says hold me and she has broken the rules in uttering two words instead of one.

    i turn and realise we have crossed the shards of glass, feet bloody and raw but nowhere near as bad as i imagined and more to the point, she is there beside me. she smiles, recognising what i have achieved.

    i hold her but she twists uncomfortably from me and grabs a tattered rag to wipe her bleeding feet.

no matter...

...we made it across.

4. the shadow

    the morning after the game, when we have both slept, elizabeth returns to me. she is wearing a string of blue-black bruises around her neck. i stare this time. i am stunned. i wonder where she went.

    elizabeth never wears her hair down, she hates it like that. instead, she fixes it with a million tiny clips, each carefully placed to hold or contain and restrain some curl or stray hair. had she let her hair fall, i would perhaps not have noticed her bruises, but even the thought of her escape is not enough to permit her to release herself from her own binds. she wears her hear up and sports her bruises. ashamed. awkward. no sense of doing it for show, that was never an issue. i feel her pain. her bruises are trying to tell me something but i cannot decipher their message because in doing so, i know that i will have to visit that place. the place of her desolation. it's taken me years to re-build myself. to take myself out of my own desolation, and although i know loneliness, and fear, and isolation still, i never want to re-visit the desolation borne of such permissiveness. the permissiveness of allowing another person to hurt you like that. to perhaps even destroy you.

at present, elizabeth manages that destruction because she is still in it. i however, cannot manage it and yes, it's true that it would destroy *me* were i to take her hand and walk with her to meet this lover who bruises her neck that way.

i stand in front of her, wanting to hold her, but she would never allow that. if i held her, she would crumble to dust. she needs me to just accept her, witness her, understand her, but never hold her or tell her she is beautiful.

elizabeth *is* beautiful. she needs to understand that. then one day she may let me hold her and smile, touch her hair and her scars. love her.

art whore

i stood there, stark bollock naked i think the saying goes, only i've got no bollocks, being a girl n'all.

i made my body a canvas and said "paint whatever you like on me; paint whatever comes to you. i want to be your muse."

he looked at me with something that looked like a cross between contempt and ferocious passion, which confused me, and picked up a handful of brushes of different sizes and shapes. behind him, there were two dozen or more glass jars, each filled with coloured liquids of different tones and consistencies.

"do you know what's in these?" he asked, "i mean, have you got any idea at all?"

"i don't care" i replied, "just paint me...please..."

"you will leave here a different woman to the one who came in asking me to do this" he continued, "so you'd better be sure. banish all doubt because i will not let you leave once i start...be careful what you wish for pretty thing."

what the fuck could i say. i couldn't back out now...i did not know how. my whole being was screaming for him to do this, without thought for the consequences. without consideration of the implications. but that was me all over. full of fire and burning desire. i looked him square in the eye.

"do it!"

the artist strode to his studio door and locked it, the heavy iron bolt clanging ominously before him. he turned to me and smiled a dark, sardonic smile. he loved me though...i knew this to be true. and he despised me for his loving me.

striding over to his great oak desk, he gathered more of his tools, a turpentine soiled rag, various painting mediums and of course those brushes and his pots of colour. he also carried a small spatula of the kind artists would use to mix oils and a yellow, plastic handled craft knife. he stood before me surveying the array of these things that meant so much to him, that defined him in this world.

in the pocket of my discarded jacket, i carried a box of bryant & may matches. i mention the brand only because you, dear reader, will understand the reliability of them. no shards of pink sulphurous remnants dropping limply to the floor when you strike a bryant & may.

he came as close to my body as he could at this point, without fucking me there and then. close enough for me to smell the cigarettes he smoked incessantly and the faint traces of his dinner. i held his gaze as he challenged me with his own.

taking one of his larger brushes, he lingered over several pots as if deciding what would be my fate, which is in fact *exactly* what he was doing. when he had chosen, he let out a deep, shuddering sigh and turned to me once again,

"no going back" he said, "no going back," and i could see that he was crying, though in a very contained manner unusual to me in my weeping, snot riddled releases.

the first stroke of that indigo dye felt cold and clammy on my bare skin, yet as he gathered his precise momentum, i felt a shift in me, subtle at first but then unmistakably familiar. i felt my head explode into a hunter's mindset and began prowling through his space and given that he did not try to stop me, would have to surmise that this was not entirely unexpected on his part....

i felt my body lithe, taut, exquisitely capable and merciless in my capacity to kill, but i was not hungry for him. there was nothing around me that i could identify as my 'home' and thus, my primal instinct to hunt was thrown into chaos. i did the only thing i knew how to do and began to pace, back and forth across his room, not knowing how to dispense this feline energy. all the time he was watching me, but he did not intervene, until the moment i walked to his artist's table and picked up the knife he had laid out. then, he in turn picked up his camcorder and began to document this subversion of my instinctive nature.

when i began to make the first light incisions across my forearms, i thought i heard him catch his breath, as if shocked by my actions, but still he did not try to stop me.

gradually that dreadful urge to harm myself, which had felt like the only possible course of action when i found myself out of my natural habitat, began to subside. when i stopped and saw myself, it was my turn to let the tears fall.

"shall we continue" he said, not waiting for my response.

i was afraid now. i had seen my first glimpse of this violent and seemingly ominous transformation from girl to muse, woman to beloved. i was not sure i could make it.

but he had warned me that he would not let me go and i did not doubt that for one moment. i summoned my gods of surrender, and i let him approach me once more, brush laden with a bright scarlet ink, the likes of which i had never seen.

"snake venom" he stated simply, and he began to paint me once again.

this time, there was no delay; the pain was instantaneous. i dropped to my knees on the spot, creased into my belly and began to writhe on the floor, begging him whilst i could still speak, to make it stop. my understanding of language and words was fading fast.

he did not move. he just stood there and watched me as i bit and bit and bit myself like some crazy malfunctioning automaton. the toxins were paralysing me. i was eating my own poison and it was threatening to kill me. i did not want to die...that wasn't part of the deal.

as the pain became unbearable, i finally let go, accepting my fate, however it came to be.

my eyes were becoming opaque, as a milky-white film descended over them and my movements began to slow. i could expend no more energy, and in spite of my burning desire to change things, i had to accept that i could not. death? does it feel this lame; this pathetic and devoid of passion?

...several moments later i stood up briskly and began to look around me. there was an old piece of snakeskin littering his floor and my whole body was painted in what seemed like a million tiny fragments of colour. when had he done this? how could that have happened? there was a landscape upon me more beautiful than any of his paintings i'd seen so far. and he, my artist was packing away his paints and colours, his brushes and his belongings. he would not turn to look at me. he could not counter what he had created upon my flesh.

with the most elegant poise i think i have ever felt in my life before that moment and since, i walked over to where my clothes lay across the arm of his chair and took out the matches. i made certain he could not hear what i was doing.

there was one fleeting split second where the realisation of what i was doing hit him as he heard that give-away spark, and yet as if in carnival style slow motion, he could not get to me in time. his canvases were so leaden with flammable mixes and so surrounded be his discarded turpentine soaked rags that they did not stands a chance. i had destroyed all of them in one instant.

he took me. i took him. there was nothing more to be said as we walked out of that place, alive and holding hands.

earthquake

when i turned around that night and saw the coppers at the door, i can honestly say, hand on heart, that i did *not* recall what had happened in those real weird moments just after he did what he'd done, and i did what i did in retaliation.

people tried to tell me i had anger management issues but let me tell you something, so would you have had fucking anger management issues if you'd been there n'all. fucking amazing he still had his insides in one long, still-put-together tennis court string if yer ask me (they say that yer know...that yer guts if they was taken out would stretch out to cover the whole of a tennis court. t'aint no picture i like to imagine fer mesel' though...bit sick if yer askin' me...)

anyhow, these days everything is kinda faint, s'a bit like the distant memory of a recurring nightmare you ain't had fer years. yer know the feelings are still locked in there somewhere; what yer saw, how yer felt, what yer did even cos yer bin told enough times so yer must'have, but the rest is a sickening blur. i say 'sickening' on account of there being (truly there is), a way my whole body gets to bein' whenever i think of that night...makes me retch up that yeller bile from some secret dark part of me. it ain't pretty neither...

now, whenever someone mentions it, or tries getting' me to talk about it, i retch just as if it were yesterday. you'd think they'd leave well enough alone now wouldn't you. i paid my dues. i did my time. why don't they let sleepin' dogs lie? vultures! vultures the fuckin' lot of 'em.

i'm gonna tell *you* though...so's you don't have ta keep askin 'me n'all and cos yer a new mate. i'm tryin' real hard to make a clean start. i think we're gonna get on yer know...don't you? you're not like them other friends i had. not one of 'em came to see me yer know...what was i sayin' then? oh yeah, well, i first heard the glass shatterin' about 1am on that windy godforsaken night. all day i'd bin testy...all fuckin' day...i'd bin tryin' real hard ta get sorted, given mesel' good talking to's, tried ta sleep, tried a bath, i'd even managed to stay off'of the ale which is pretty fucking amazing for me. anyways...i'd gone up, somweheres around about midnight i guess it must'ha been, thinkin' sleep might ha been the best thing for it really, an' then some time later i heard it. i heard it before i knew what was was comin' an'all...that was the worst bit, that waitin'....knowin'....

he whole house was shakin' an me, well i sat bolt upright in me bed an' i knew, just knew that he'd come for me. i crept downstairs in my pretty new robe, adrenalin pumping like a greedy john after a year without pussy...well i saw the window gaping open, smashed into jarred little bits all over the floor right there in fronta me and my only puzzle was where the fuck was he? i din't like knowin' that, havin' spent years keepin' one step ahead of him.

well, night was as black as pitch an' when i looked outta that broken window but what the fuck d'ya think i saw then hey? (an tell me this wouldn't fuck with your head n'all...), well there was three men all doin' this real strange dance and getting' closer and closer all the time. one of em, when i got to see 'em up a bit closer was that stupid fuck who i'd gone out with once but the other two i din't know from jack. they looked like clowns, dancin' fuckin' clowns was all i could see, so i starts laughin'…well yer would wouldn't yer?

as i'm laughin there, one of em puts his face right up close to me and next thing i knew, i was bleedin' from me hands. lots of it too…i'd got distracted with them crazy dancers and he must'ha snuck up on me from behind like he always did, well when i looked down there was bright scarlet pools of blood drippin' down my new robe which made me mad as hell. first off i thought it was his blood but then i saw it was mine. he had a blade chopping right deep into my fingers an i couldn't believe i hadn't felt it till now as two of em were damn near hangin' off. that cunt meant business.

well…some kali-like spirit must'ha bin with me yer know cos somehow, don't even ask me cos i don't know, i got the bastard off'of me, looked up at them dancing clowns and then that was it…the rest is gone.

coppers came for me. kids got taken away (still can't see 'em unless i'm with some fucking self-righteous social worker and lord knows i was only doin' my best by 'em and what any mother'd do) and i got banged up for a ten stretch.

these days i keep better company n'all….people like you who know how to let me be, men who treat me like a lady and not some two-bit whore. only yesterday one just bought me a pretty ring an' said he don't want nothin' for it…fancy that…nothin' at all….

i'm on me way up i am….bet yer you're happy for me, nah?

mental

i had to get out. i had to leave. the lock-in started at 5pm; after that there would be no chance.

so far, i'd been spat on, verbally abused, treated like a fucking child, expected to eat the most disgustingly unimaginative food on earth (you're sick...what do you expect, gourmet cuisine?), attached to limpet-style by some woman who decided i was her salvation (may the gods help her) and offered ot, which in their language stands for 'occupational *t*herapy' but in mine stands for '*o*h look a *t*wat approaches.'

i had to get out.

i was sitting there minding me own business like, the sickly yellow walls adding to my malaise, the thin brown carpet sending rivers of static up my legs, when this woman came and sat right down beside me. seventy if she was a day.

she goes "give me your teddy bear!"

to which i reply "get lost would you."

cos that's how you talk in there. hard hitting, no frills, survival of the fittest, and besides, what the fuck does some seventy year old woman want with my teddy bear...i've had it since i was two, it keeps my secrets, she could just fuck right off she could.

she goes "give me your teddy bear" again, in some flat largactyl-laden monotone, doped to the high heavens but clearly not high enough, and so i go "fuck off will you," this time. clear. concise. no messing.

she leans across me, catches me unawares and rips the bear from my lap. she begins to cradle it softly in her arms, starts to sing. fer fucks sake man...

"give me the bear back old lady," i say.

she carries on singing. then, this dark caul falls over her face. terry the tramp, who has witnessed all of this goes, "oh-oh," and moves sideways fast. i watch him, bemused. inexperienced. the dark caul falls as quick and clear as a thundercloud in the moments before rainfall and everything becomes luminous in that surreal, luminous, greener-than-grass kind of way you get before a storm hits.

"you're mental you," i say to her.

"shut the fuck up," says terry the tramp.

"tell you what, why don't you shut the fuck up," i reply.

meantime, grandma over there starts growling under her breath and starts fucking ripping the stuffing out of my bear! no fucking way...i am raging now. i've had that bear since i was two...did i say that already? and if it can survive my father kicking it around my five year old's bedroom floor just out of spite, then no fucking doped-up grannie is getting hold of it now. it's seen me through my smack addiction that bear. it's borne witness to secrets and lies. it knows me. she is destroying it.

i stand and terry the tramp shouts "fucking move! now!" and then it all happens so fast. i reach for the bear, my bear in the same freaky moment that this frail but clearly not so frail old lady lifts the enormous coffee table in front of us, way up over her head.

"neyyyyyyuuuuuurrrgggggghhhhhhhhhh," she howls as she looks me in the eye and heaves the table straight at my head.

i move swiftly. faster than i thought i could given i was sick. her, she looks like the devil lives inside of her. she is serious in her desire to do me harm. i am her long lost son. my bear was her baby for a moment and when he grew up and left, i became her boy and she had to kill me. this is what terry the tramp tells me after everything has calmed down and a gaggle of frenzied nurses have restrained her then carted her off for more ect. i can't bear to see them when they come back. their soul is gone. why do they do that? why do they anaesthetize the spirit of a person in the name of medicine and health?

i go to the women's toilets and i am sick. i throw up my guts into the pristine ceramic bowl. the relief of that table not hitting my head, the fear, the moment of five year old panic when my bear was in her arms, the confusion, the loss, the deep, deep sorrow on seeing that woman come back from the ect room, devoid of anything. she had a slight dribble of spit running from the left hand corner of her mouth. that made me cry.

it was mental in there.

mental

razor

i pushed my key into the rusty lock and proceeded to do the usual irritating dance, this way and that, until the fucking thing decided to grant me access to my own bloody home. it was ten in the morning, i was shivering with cold and pissed off with the perpetual damp manchester air. rain, rain, rain….cold, tight, mean-spirited weather. i hated it like this….really fucking hated it.

under normal circumstances, normal late winter mornings, my body would be tighter than an unforgiving clam, only this was no normal winter morning. i had recently discovered something that was keeping me alive and my urgency to get the front door open, to get in, was more about following this discovery than about getting warm. housework piled up around me. bills needed paying. things needed attending to left, right and centre but i really didn't give a damn today.

i dialed the number, my palms sweating profusely as i did so; "i'm ready" i said, and replaced the telephone into its little curved nest.

i walked upstairs and set out the things i needed. the camcorder was charged. the razorblade was sharp and clean, the antiseptic wipes were carefully placed beside the glinting silver blade. there were two black velvet ties on either side of my bed. he would bring the rest.

i checked myself in the mirror. tight black pencil skirt, accentuating my woman's hips. snugly fitted red sweater forcing the eye to my full and still pretty breasts. shiny natural nylons and stupidly high black patent leather heels. i liked this look. it spoke to me of promise and filth. it said slut, and i celebrated that fact. i was tired of playing good girl to anyone else's judgment.

i had to fight not to begin before he arrived. i could feel my whole body and soul yearning for it to start. like an imprint it was, a deep and relentless imprint.

by the time i heard my mobile buzzing its silent-set alert, i was almost on the verge of tears; salty, terrified, excited tears.

"let me in" was all he said.

i had never met him before, though i knew his face and his ways. he both intrigued and scared me. he was trustworthy. i could afford no less than perfection here. there was too much to lose; too much at stake.

"this way" i whispered, my voice suddenly unable to extend beyond a hoarse and limited ripple across the scale of him. he was huge, his stature captivated my imagination. naturally, he was scarred all over and appeared to me to be the most self-contained dignified man i had ever met, but he was sick, or so others would have me believe.

i knew better. i had intelligence, discretion, the power of choice. i knew myself well. i pushed my boundaries in the quest for art and creativity. i wanted to be consumed by them. here was my demon. he was my enabler, for sure.

i took him upstairs into my loft room and watched as he surveyed my personal space. he laid down his coat, a heavy black woolen crombie, folding it meticulously on my red leather chair in the corner.

i found him fascinating.

he nodded. i responded by walking slowly to my bed, which he had covered in a thin latex sheet of a beautiful pale duck egg blue, and i began to undress; shy in front of this stranger to whom i was entrusting myself.

by the time i stood naked, self conscious in my unclothed state beside his fully dressed body, i was shivering and my teeth were chattering, but not from the cold...

i lay down and let a single tear fall from my eye as i tried desperately to stem the flow of more, which would of course betray me. i held out my wrists as let him bind me to the black metal posts of my bed. he began to bind my ankles, working swiftly in order to diminish the opportunity for fear or wavering confidence.

by the time he had made the first cut, i could no longer contain my tears and i wept and wept and wept. he continued, knowing exactly what he was there for. by body was alive; after a half hour or so, it was stinging so much that i could barely breathe and yet the design he was forming was mine...only mine, and my breathless pain was all part of this ritual and would undoubtedly become a vital part of my remembering.

i hit orgasm just as he made the final incision. he released my binds, picked up his coat and was gone before i even realised where i was. taken far beyond my recognition and all that felt familiar, i had exceeded my own sense of possibility and become, in that moment, the artist i knew i was.

my skin bore the raised, bloody red whelts that marked this to be my truth.

i had found an immense power that could only drive me further into my heart and my purpose in this life.

and i had fallen in love with myself on that day.

sideshow medicine

by the time i got home from that freezing cold, stranded-out-in-the-middle'a-nowhere walk home, i realised that i'd managed to walk to some other house that didn't even belong to me. i'd gone into auto-pilot, following a small trail of blood on the pavement (it seemed as good a lead as any in my whisky riddled state).

i realised, like i said, that the house i now stood outside wasn't actually mine. i stood at the front window and pressed my nose up against the glass. i figured that seeing as how it musta been somewhere like 5:00am and seeing as how it was the mother of all winter nights, that no-one would notice me and think me strange. everyone would be fast asleep in their planet cosyland dream homes with their planet cosyland dream lovers and dream children. me, i was lost.

you know what...i don't even know how long i stood there before i knocked. i could sorta see myself doing something ridiculous...knocking on a stranger's door. i'd no idea what i would say, or to whom, but i just knew i had to knock.

a woman came to the door....thank god it was a woman!

"save me?" i whispered, and i looked her straight in the eye. i was searching. she twitched. a tiny, almost indiscernible tic above her top lip. she hadn't decided what to do or what to say to me yet. she weighed me up a moment longer, meeting my gaze.

"why?"

"i'm not sure" i said "i think i need you to save me though. i stopped at your house didn't i. it's as good a place as any to start and your house must've had *something* that drew me here."

she stepped aside, indicating to me that i could enter. she never took her eyes off me.

she ushered me towards another room. from the faint remains of an odour of bitter curry, i guessed it was her kitchen she was sending me to. the heart of a woman's home, unless she's a whore, then it would be her bedroom. her bedroom would be her refuge or her income. this was the kitchen though. i guessed that this woman probably had kids and probably wasn't a whore. i followed behind her, surveying her belongings as if there were an announcement of some kind on every single thing, like 'this coat is the one he gave me last winter; i hate it now he's gone but it's too cold to throw it out at this time of year,' or 'this china vase used to hold flowers held in lovers hands or bought as peace offerings from errant kids or platitudes from my mother.'

i invented stories about her in that short journey from front door to kitchen and i knew she was not going to let me down. she invited me in didn't she.....

armed and extremely dangerous

you ask too much of me i say. your demands are too great.

i ask nothing of you, you reply, your impressions are false.

you leave me no choice i say, your expectations are immense.

i expect nothing. you give me nothing. i am not disappointed then. you pretend.

inside, a tiny heart beats and threatens to bust its blood red guts all over my pillow, but instead it leaves silver trails of semen all over my sheets. they are easier to ignore. they are easier to clean up.

inside, a cheap whore laughs and cavorts with angels. she is the whore of babylon and a vessel for all to fill with their own desire. she accommodates everything and everyone and hides when dawn breaks. nightfall is her time. she is beautiful. she shines bright and her shimmering facade scares many. they cannot contemplate their own whore. their own demons. their own angels hold them in eternal torment and lies because they got them so wrong. they never learned how to translate 'light' and so they became new-age and new-man and nouveau riche and new-born and new shiny shiny squeaky afraid of their own tongues and cunts and fiery bellies.

she, she rides on the back of the beast and play with it as if it were her pet. mostly, it responds well to her; occasionally it bites her, which makes her cry.

when you began to communicate with her, you feel in love with her. when you began to fornicate with her, you began to fear her. when you began to fear her, you began to contain her. and she began to weep. you hated her for weeping. you hated her weakness. you mistook it for softness when in fact it was strength. you tried to lock her in a gilded cage and she wept even more. she began to disappear and her pet came looking for her. you heard its wailing cry and your body crumbled, bent in terror at the prospect of her revenge on its lonely behalf. so you tried to finish her off. with words. her own weaponry used against her. that was real clever...real clever....but she, she is the whore of babylon and she cannot be fooled for she has lost everything already.

she lost everything ten times over and you, you teach her about love and about fear and about the amount of pain she has borne and can bear. she loves you for that alone. though she loves you for much more.

you are the harlot's plaything. she lifts her skirts and reveals that she is armed and extremely dangerous.

brown

julie's dead. manni's dead. patsy's dead. her twin (patsy's that is) sister jean survived, though in all likelihood she will be dead by now too. sad really. they were all right ya know.

when julie smiled, her teeth were a right mess, so she did that thing where whenever she actually did crack a smile, she employed so many facial muscles to protect her face from revealing her broken, black teeth that she ended up looking kinda twisted and wrong. she shoulda just smiled and to hell with it cos you could always see those rotten teeth, and the contortions of her face just ended up accentuating them really.

manni was short. only five seven or so, with greasy limp black hair that hung in straight rods down either side of his ears and cheeks, plastered to his face with a mix of sweat, natural oils and dirt. he rarely left his bed, which he lay on top of 24/7 except to go to the toilet or weigh out his gear. didn't want the rest of us to see those two, though i think he'd have been less bothered about us seeing him piss and shit than about us seeing his gear. shrewd but in truth, not cut-throat enough to be a dealer. too human, too soft, too hooked. manni used to grouch all day long on that dirty fucking bed, the twins sitting on the threadbare sofa to his left hand side. the bitter reassuring smell of burning brown ever in the air. it stank in there but it stank of drugs and those who came there liked it that way. made you feel safe. as long as it stank that way, there was gear around.

patsy was a strange creature. she wore her hair long, usually tied back in a ponytail on account that she'd managed to set fire to it too many times when cookin' up her gear. brown, long, unfussed hair. mousy i think you call it. just like her. unobtrusive, sweet and so close to her twin that the pair of them could freak you out easily as anything with their simultaneous expression or knowing. they would just operate like one person really. until patsy died. and jean, having been manni's lover too, lost two of the people she loved most in the world. two of the people who made sense of everything for her, even if it was only in some tiny basement flat that stank of gear and months of neglect.

jean was always the strongest of the three of them (manni, patsy and her). she, i think, kept it together. she, i think, told manni how to deal, when to deal, when to hit, where to hit (so's his veins didn't collapse or his arms burst up like christmas balloons again). you'd know that jean would always keep some of their stuff to one side so that when the scarce times hit, they'd be okay for another hit at least. the dealers needed to keep it together that bit longer in case they had to go out and score. the junkies would just call and call and call, begging them to share it, accusing them of stashing it, cursing them for their callous lack of understanding. it's everyone for themselves when there's no gear love. surely you know that by now? jean outlived her sister and her lover but there was nothing left for her when they'd gone. nothing at all.

julie saw everything. she knew what she had to do to survive and she did it. her kid was generally taken care of, she didn't let him see much. her habit was massive though, and it had taken most of her teeth. she was the kind of junkie carried an ever present sadness, never wanted anyone else to go through what she did, even as she was doing it, so she never ever tried to take you down with her like most junkies did. she would watch carefully behind her piercing, glazed over, bright blue eyes, and tell you not to do that. not to go there. no, i will not dig you for a hit girl, you can do it yourself. i'll never be the one who takes you there. stay on the smoke baby. don't start on the needles. she saved me. that maltese angel saved me. she was riddled with gear and sorrow. her heart was big. her sense of right and wrong was strong. i remember her with respect, that broken toothed junkie.

manni had a big heart too. maybe it was his undoing? who knows. only in that world could a big heart kill you. or maybe that's not true....

jean was more ruthless. patsy was lost.

tony, in another scene, well he was kind of different. different drugs, different people. freebase ('crack' only nobody called it that in those days) got a different class of dealer back then. more of the upper class boys gone bad. crack houses now...well it's all madness and fucked-up heroes again. tony was a mystery to me. i never really knew him but you couldn't get two more different vibes. one all spaced out and stinking of bitter almond brown; one all tense and tight with that sweet acrid smell of burning white rocks and an eagle eye from every person in the room, checking to see if someone took more than their time on that pipe. junkies wouldn't have known or cared about anything like that. too fucking stoned.

how many of them died from the gear? how many of them died from other shit? how many of them are left? we all die sooner or later, from something or other.

dancing queen
my life according to the gospel of abba

i stood on the deck of that boat, my skirt-tails dripping the salty water of the ocean's tide as i set sail for foreign places and faraway dreams. in my head at least, i was free. in my head at least, i was on the greatest adventure of all time. i was making ready to dive into deep waters.

in actual fact, the salty water dripping from my petticoats was the residue of your last ejaculate as it dripped in full, heavy return down the inside of my thigh. i was not setting sail, more bound to the mast, and i was not in faraway lands, i was in the kitchen, doing the dishes or something dull and mundane like that.

but inside my head, i was the dancing queen.

inside my head, i was the freedom fighter.

inside my head, the cum that dripped down my leg cost *you* more than it cost *me*, but we both know that was a lie.

i slept deeply that night. my dreams crackling in and out like the static on a nylon shirt on washday. i saw your fear and it was huge. you saw my vulnerability and it left you cold. a serpent's eye surveying the last kill. ruthless. calculated. precise. me, i was all over the fucking place. but then perhaps you were too.

your love undid me. i knew it would. i saw it coming. i had to be prepared to rip myself open and let go in the name of that love. if i'd known it would hurt this much, would i have done so? would i have taken myself to that cross and yelled "nail me up baby" like i was now? in my own head that is. in my own head.

in my own head i am a super trooper.

in my dreams, knowing me, knowing you, i may have had more wisdom, but the heart will always rule the head in my artist's world and my passion for true love will always prevail. blindfold, you lead me down a dark alley. blindfold i lead you down into the dark belly of the earth where you despise the cold touch of that dank, dark soil upon your skin. the darkness disturbs you. i am at home.

i look around and scattered at my bloody feet are the souls who would save me. amongst others, mary magdelene; prostitute, bathing my feet as if they were her own. they *are* her own. she weeps for all of the men who think they possessed her. she knows better than that. a brief rental income does not a possession make, love possessed her though, just as love possesses me.

i work all night, i work all day, i pay the bills i have to pay, ain't it sad. and still there never seems to be, a single thing you left for me...money, money, money. everything so clear, so calculated, so detached. it's a rich man's world. and in my dreams at least, i make a living that is more than scratching around in the dirt for your crumbs.

still, i dance amongst stars, offering up prayers for my healing, for my life, for my spirit.

foreplay or obituary

"can you ever forgive me?" i said.

"what, for doing what you did to me?" he said.

"no, for not wiping my boots properly on the mat on my way in" i said, "i can see that you're very proud of this new carpet baby..."

he looked me square in the eye. "you're a cunt!" he said.

"i'm working on it" i replied.

then we ran out of conversation.

it was uncomfortable in the extreme. i wanted cigarettes and whisky. he wanted women and love. he wanted to be wanted. i wanted to be free. i wanted to be wanted too, though he never expressed a desire to be free. he, on the other hand, kept tight to his routines and gazed at me with some quizzical sense of absolute alienation. who are you? who am i? what the fuck were we?

i took off my boots and lay them at his feet, which instantly improved things.

"clean them" i said.

he picked them up and went for the polish. there was no question that he wouldn't do it.

"fuck me" i said, but the command lingered silent as a church bell on sunday morning.

"you're still a cunt" he said.

"i'm really not" i replied, "you just don't know me." he laughed. i lit up another cigarette, despite the fact that *he* was the smoker. he sat beside me and took my hand in his. his hands were so familiar. the hairs on the back of them; the way his thumbs curled back more than mine. the way he held his cigarettes. the way he fucked me with those hands. the ring on his baby finger that i bought him, to make peace after a particularly nasty argument. he kept it on even after i had taken off my own. he always needed the last word.

he rested his arm across the end of the purple sofa we bought together, avoiding my skin, my flesh; the electricity of me. it was awkward, but safer that way. those arms that i knew so well. every last hair. every tiny blush of redness on his elbows. every bite in his muscular upper arms. his shoulders. they made me want to cry when they were so hell bent on avoiding touching me. i knew if he did though, that we were sunk again.

so he crossed his legs in adverse body language. those legs that i knew so well. every slight bend and every slight turn and every way in which they gripped hold of me when we fucked, drawing me in, ever closer, trying to consume me. succeeding.

"please cover your legs" i said, "they are disturbing me." he did *not* go to put on long trousers though, intent upon tormenting me it seemed.

"wipe your boots next time!" he said.

flight

charred and blackened remains lay littered around my feet/talons. talons being french for high heels. feet being bound in japan. charred and black being the debris of a life once lived, all burnt to the ground now…all gone. teetering and bound, i wait patiently for flight.

i preen my new feathers and wonder how i got to be here, high above the city for this moment only at least, in the crumbling old window frame of an ancient building long since abandoned. there are gargoyles all around me; whenever i move, their eyes, static, cold, ruthlessly still, seem to follow me. but i don't care, for i am free. and i have known the residue and lingering, clinging pain of coldness for too long now to let any inanimate object disturb me. the warm blooded are far more ruthless than any imaginary creature. far more…

you tried to eat me yesterday. i almost let you. devoured would be a more fitting word. you tried to devour me and leave only bones and remnants of bloody skin around you, hoping that no-one would notice your ugly sin. you were licking your lips before you even started. i, being a sensory creature, sniffed out the blood lust in you and took flight before you sunk in your perfectly honed teeth. you; you were powerless to steal that from me, for you were cemented to your principles so long ago, and they are heavy burdens to bear.

i became falcon again this morning. sometimes it happens without my knowing. one moment human, then in an instant shape-shifting into a new form. this one, like snake, terribly familiar to me. i let cry the whoop of the falcon in flight, in hunting mode, and i felt my wings expanding out of my spine, bursting out of my flesh in a way that i will never get used to. it will always pain me, though like childbirth, as a necessary means to an end and thus endured.

i am grateful for this gift. i am grateful for the power of flight. those who are envious try to convince me that flying is bad. that enduring is better. those who know the freedom of flight circle above me sending out their cries, hoping i will remember my essence and fly again. when the moment arrives, the inevitable occurs and my wings will no longer remain bound to my previous form. then, and only then, i feel the painful pleasure of release, of a greater being than myself. some call it god, others the devil. some call it witchcraft, others redemption.

for me, it is salvation and i am grateful for it...this gift...this bloody and painful salvation.

this flight.

jellyfish

when i was a child, we would go to the beach after a storm and poke at jellyfish. we would take a long stick and prod them to make sure they were dead, that they could no longer sting us; hurt us. their placid pink, lilac, semi-transparent forms lying devoid of all power would delight us, though secretly we still believed (privately and without admitting it to the other) that they could, at any given moment, rise up and catch our bare feet with a flailing tentacle.

they would lie. dead. washed into movement by the odd surge of a tide. we would run, and scream, and be thankful that they did not catch at our heels or our fleshy children's toes. i was fascinated by them. at once so deadly, and then ravaged and rendered impotent.

you prod at me. you stare. i lie, lifeless but not dead. and yet *i* am the child running. *you* hold the stick and you poke and poke at me until i think death would in fact be preferable to this endless humiliating probing. i hold still and guard my tentacles close to my shape-shifting form. let the tide carry me. let the waves take me. let the form bruise and mold me at the same time.

i cannot fight against your arsenal of seaside weapons.

early on in this story i recall for a moment a time when i felt your barb implanted deep, deep under my dermis. it began to spread like an alien invader and i, being a sentient creature, gathered my troops and released into my ailing body, an army of white cell protectors. it was futile. one cannot fight the tides of love, for love is based upon faith, hope and illusion and all of these are bigger than me; bigger than any army i could hope to summon to counteract you. i was powerless. i told myself stories. fairytales. superheroes were dispatched to rescue me.

jellyfish.

when i was a child, there were sharks under my bed and my dressing gown, hanging on the back of my bedroom door was 'monster'. they frequently consumed me. i later learned that not everyone battled such demons, where i had thought them commonplace. you came to me and presented a monster of unfamiliar guise and i hated you for that. i had not the tools to fight you. you gained access to my inner world, for i loved you. i would have given everything to discover that the monster that was you was in fact looking for laughs, and that i was a deluded child who had yet again mistaken the familiar for the deadly. but my love suspended all disbelief and i simply grinned at you at waited for your arms to hold me, telling myself that i was no longer a child and that monsters were not real; that they never were.

but they are.

and they creep in and make ready to battle with every superhero i could ever invent. they don't necessarily inflict fatal damage, it's true, but their barbs leave a residue that perhaps becomes part of us eventually.

wise men apparently say "that which does not kill you, makes you stronger," to which i reply, "did i tell you that when i was a child we used to search out jellyfish on the beach after a storm, just so that we could finally hold power over that which ever threatened to destroy our pleasure of an untamed surf?"

you sigh and think me a lost cause.

i lie pink and formless, allowing you to prod and prod until the night falls and a graceful tide washes me back into my home.

a manchester tale

drunk, weaving down the rain spattered manchester streets, dodging the fucking "piss on her for fun" cars, i was home, but was this it - was this everything?

the lights flickered, broken, stinking of the piss of the night people, shedding pathetic remnants of synthetic power. not so grand now, when casting shadows over my sorry face, my soaked-to-the-scalp hair, heavy, black, false-lash-effect mascara run eyes hiding the tears. i live here. i am home. i wanted this. i love this. it's perverse but i fucking love this place.

half an hour earlier, my feet stuck to the sorry red carpets, each time i lifted a stiletto it squelched a yearning for me to stay in the one spot. 'don't go' it begged, i wanna fuck with you, i wanna watch you gettin buried in this corner, on this spot, making my mark, in remembering you, in you remembering me.

remembering you....there's a tune in my head and it makes me cry....i see your face and i remember gigs and dirty coaches, riders of wild turkey and twanging guitar strings tuning up. i remember my friend running around lamp posts on a busy london street, chasing you, you in your beige raincoat, as you sang "remembering you, fingertips on red rose lips...." and we laughed because we were relatively carefree then, despite our stories. they were minnows in comparison to the ones we tell now.

i remember you because my story became your story, because of photographs on blackpool beaches. i remember you because you didn't make it and i did. your sweet soul voice as haunting now as it was then; bittersweet now.

manchester. my city. the junkies and the whores. the thieves and the djs. the bullets and the books. the musicians and the money. the artists and the samaritan callers lining up to be heard. and i sink another whisky in remembrance of everywhere i walked, of every dream i dreamt. tib street. fleeing the grasp of the one violator and swapping it for the next. pink nylon sheets on "ooh aaah" faked pleasures, paying my rent with them. paying the price.

i look up into the rain now as it gets heavier and heavier. i open my mouth and drink in the beautiful water. acid rain? i smile into the cracked lights and the moonlit city skies. i smile into the fucking rain and let the cars screech past, bellowing their cruel laughter at my expense because none of it matters. love is all that matters, and you love me and i love you.

i stagger further on and pull of my crippling shoes. fuck it! i shove them into my bag and surrender to the downpour. once you're wet there comes a point where you can't get any wetter, and where as my mother says when she quotes her lyrical piecemeal "been down so long it looks like up to me."

my body maps my story, my face tells who i am. my masks are dropped and i no longer care for them. all of us are scattered into the wind now doing our fucking best to stay alive, to stay cripplingly beautiful, and from where i stand, whisky-drenched and wet, we're doing pretty fucking well.

and you mister dj...did you save my life last night? did you play me the ultimate record? will you sing me the ultimate song? you are forever part of my story and it is a manchester love story, for we are home here.

this story is dedicated to Bryan Glancy 1966-2006,

amputation

i dragged on my makeup, what little i wore these days, no point cos i'm that feckin' plain anyway. pulled down that stupid red hat onto my unruly fucked up hair. 4am and i was due in work in half an hour; takes me three quarters to get there. bastard boss would be on my case all day now.

i got this job because it was better'n the last one where that cunt of a boss used to grope us all day. any old excuse, but never quite plain enough to make a case against it. passin' to collect something from behind us, askin' us to put something in the back for his girlfriend (the poor cow) and then huggin' us for doing so, though his hands always where they shouldn't 'a been when he 'thanked' us. even his girlfriend asked if my tits were real once and then helped herself to a feel. me, i left when his groping came more obvious cos i knew it were only a matter of time fore he got *really* nasty. like i sad, i ain't a pretty girl neither, it's harder for me to fight them kinda things...no-one tends to believe ugly girls or plain girls. it's like why would some fucker go for *you*, you desperate old bitch when his girlfriend was right good looking n'all. dunno is the answer to that...don' ask me....power i guess.....but fuck! it made my job a pain in the ass.

the day i did leave, he cornered me in the back stock room and started askin' me why i was goin' an that. i said "dunno sir" and tried to get outta there fast. he came to hug me, to say 'goodbye properly' as he put it. my heart sank. i felt his hand up the side of my thigh, rubbing closer to the top of my leg, movin t'ward the middle where my underclothes meet the crease in my groin. he had one finger tryin' to press into them panties i swear. i shoved him hard and he said "fucking cow! get out of here and don't expect a reference!"

   i started at the bagel store next door the week after that. i would'ha taken that twat to court only i knew what would happen. i've only got one leg see. amputated the other after a freak accident about ten years back. i shouldn'ta known where his hand was see; no leg there an all, and they'd have laughed me out of court. i still feel everything in that leg even tho it ain't there. everything still lingers. the pain of it never goes away.

dirty love

she planted a seed of an idea in my head that grew hotter than georgia tarmacadam. it burned me up soon as i let it filter into my imagination. i was known for my fanciful ways.

i loved that woman and her telling me that, well it was kinda inevitable that it would take hold of me that way. a kind of chilli and fire yearning mixed in with a dark foreboding sense of unquenchable longing; a recipe for disaster.

she of course remained blameless throughout the trial. it was never gonna fall on her, the responsibility. shoulda been a law about ethical responsibility if ya ask me, only nobody did ever ask me, cosi was painted the harlot right from the start. in fact, you could say it was a loaded gun that trial, a loaded gun jes' waiting to be fired and it was pointing straight at me. i wasn't no fool. i knew it. i accepted it. i loved her regardless.

she got me to clean up after her; i knew that now. that man had hurt her real bad but i, ever the innocent didn't even know she knew him when i first met him. she however, had carefully orchestrated our meeting with the attention to detail one might expect from a small-time bookie protecting his payouts. nothing was left to chance. everything was fixed. i was merely a pawn, though i believe she loved me too, but she was a mercenary bitch, and i, well i was a naive distraction.

she had wept tears of razor blade sharpness in her desire for a different outcome with him. she had stalked him for a while but nothing changed. he would not accept her. could not fathom her. he had chosen 'sweet' over edgy. he had chosen control over freedom. freedom was too chaotic for him and so he chose to loathe her and to resent the threat she posed. he despised her because it was easier that way. lazy. fucking. cunt.

dead. manipulated. lover.

hopeless. innocence. forsaken.

i had loved her as she had loved him. i would have done anything for her; well i *did* do anything. i paid the ultimate price. not the jail. not the guilt. but the unacceptable face of love's longing unmet. i had to live with that. fuck that i killed a man. fuck that i had lost my liberty. i...i had to live with the longing of unrequited love and the knowledge that i had been used. that alone would have been sentence enough, though not in the court's eyes and never in hers. she remained conveniently blind. her lover was dead. she no longer had to live with this gnawing yearning that she had handed to me. clever of her to pass me the stick and run. clever of her to absolve herself of her sins. i loved her for her wit, her charm, her intelligence so how could i hate her for proving it to me.

i was the fool. the tarot told me. my friends told me. the voice my mother taught me never to ignore told me. i'm fucking innocent officer. my only crime is love.

salman and stell

"feck!...stell...you see that?! thatfecker there was salman rushdie! i kid you not...driving that car jespickin his nose, brazen as anything the dirty ole git!"

"don't be schtoooooopidsyl" she says "salman rushdie don drive round here in some fucking silver ford fiesta pickin his nose!"

"nah but man, i swear it was and he looked mean man, tiny little shark eyes lookin like they was gunnin for somethin he wan't gettin an all. i don like it stell, i smell a rat."

and i left it there cos stell wasn't having none of it, and i, syl, knew better.
so we keeps driving till we get to that lock-up and park up on the side of the road, you know, two wheels on the kerb to make sure our place was well ours like. i go "are you sure about this stell? it's been a while," and she goes "yeah syl, just chill will ya, yer making me feckin nervous," and i whispers under me breath so's not to make her mad "yeah well maybe you should be feckin nervous..."

i follows her down that alleyway, them cobbles really messin with my heels which was pissin me off already and i wan't happy about it i can tell ya. i di'n even want to come here on this feckingoos chase, an if yer ask me a goose chase is exactly what it was. laying ghosts to rest stell called it tho feck knows what *that* meant. stell goes quiet suddenly, she looks up and i see her eyes is all glassy pretendin she ain't cryin but i knows stell,

"y'alright doll?" i asks her.

she don answer.

she pulls an old rusty key out of her pocket.

"feck me you daft bitch! whered'you get that and what the feck makes you think that'll work now you silly cunt?!"

"i love you too syl" she says drily and then walks toward that door like the promise of an eternity in good shoes an easy livin was held in there.

but she was a whore and whores don't get fairy tales right? she wrote about her story you know, my mate stell. she only goes and gets feckin telly and papers and all that stuff ringin and knockin and callin no end. they go "but miss accrington, what do you say to those who argue that you are condoning prostitution in the telling of your story?" and stell goes "we are all prostitutes" or some deep shit like that.

i love her. she is so feckin cool that bird!
her key turns! i *hear* it feckin turn. she's in. she drops to her knees and weeps. she takes out matches and a tin of lighter fuel from the other pocket and i think 'shit! this is gonna go feckin tits-up any minute,' so i says ;

"stell...don'!" and she goes, calm as a feckin cucumber "shut the fuck up syl!"

so i do. i know when that bird means business.

she leaves a trail then lights it on her way out. everything in that dried up crusty ole place goes up quick as a whore gets a dick up on a busy night.
"condone that motherfuckers!" she says and turns to leave.

"feck stell! that's bad. that's really bad!"

"best get out then hey" she goes an winks at me!

i swear now, no word of a lie, that as we leave and go back to our cars, there he was, that writer bloke gettin out of his ford fiesta an starin her right in the eye.

stell goes "mr rushdie, what is your view of censorship?" as those flames lick hard behind us. she has the matches in her hand.

and he goes "we are all prostitutes miss accrington"

and i just think to mesel, 'feckin hell, salman rushdie knows stell!'

soul retrieval

my fingernails were splitting as i dug. my knuckles bled, my knees becoming bulbous and a dark blue-red blotchy mass of dimpled skin as they struggled to support me in my explorations. i needed to remain still, in that one position to focus my resolution to find it. it was as hungry as i to find its way back to me.

i sat atop my bent knees weeping as i buried my hands deep into that cold, damp earth; snot and tears mixed freely upon my cheeks and the narrow passageway between my nose and mouth. i had felt your kisses on those snot riddled lips only hours before; had you seen me as i looked now you may not have been so eager to explore my face with your probing tongue. you may not have felt the bloody yearning had it been covered in this ugly mess, and not sanitised with delicate sprays of feminine perfumes and lace edged lingerie. here i was, digging frantically in the moonlight, under the beech tree in that clearing where i once buried this piece of myself, fanciful that i would never again visit this place. at the time, believing i had found all i needed to be whole, this part of me extradited into the keeping of the ancient tree at whose roots i now dug.

the mulch of the winter leaves was freezing the parts of my body that i was too driven by my desire to find this treasure to have covered appropriately. my skirt hitched up around my thighs to afford a better position for my obsessive search. i stopped for a moment to wipe the sweat from my forehead, which had been dropping into my eyes and stinging me with salty viciousness. the mud on the back of it streaked the smell of the damp earth into my ragged lined brow and i inhaled deeply of earth's rich and delightful odour. instinctively i touched my cunt at the same time, connecting the primal smell to the primal action. i let my neck drop back and strangled a deep, retching sob which was threatening to throw my concentration off the task at hand. i had to find it. i knew it had to come back to me.

one hour earlier i had left my warm bed, still ripe with the smell of you, having dreamt of snake teaching me, showing me that there had been another skin to shed. i dreamt of the tree, i saw myself here. i went deep into the roots of her and entered a dreamscape of thick black tar where nothing moved or flowed, its essence in the wounds of my past, the wounds of your past. i saw myself splitting and saw snake inside me, in the channel of my upright axis, giving me the huge strength i needed to do this. reclaim yourself he told me. reclaim yourself.

so here i found myself in this night-time clearing, alone, bloody, dirty, stripped of everything and with nothing more to lose. visions of your body flashing in front of me. flickers of your arms, your touch, your movement, the remembrance of your presence making me weep for our pain.

and then i found it.

it was exactly as i'd left it except for the damp which had invaded its core and the odd trace of mildew which had sprouted on its surface. nothing too irreparable. nothing too alarming. i held it in my hands, fascinated.

took a torch to it, examined it, allowed it to baffle me. was this really mine? had i really left it here, a solitary abandoned thing, thinking i was leaving it in safe guardianship? it had been well protected regardless. the tree, the earth, the solid wooden box in which i'd placed it more reliable than ever i could have been at that time. i felt a trickle of something run down my hand and it was then that i noticed that this thing, this treasure of mine, was bleeding. a pulsing twitch running across one side had ripped a tiny fissure from which a dark red blood was now pumping out with a rhythm of steady predictability.

i held it to my face, it comforted me. the tears began to fall more slowly now. a steady acceptance of loss and longing.

it was then that i began to eat my own heart. it was then that i knew the time had come, and i sat in that clearing in the dark night sky, under the light of a near full moon, bloody, snotty, dirt covered and undone.
and i ate my own heart.

i ate every last fragment, taking care to leave nothing of it behind.

cautious

cautious...i needed to be very cautious. i had committed the act over six months ago and yet there was a recent change in the wind that unsettled me. the perfume of my deed had turned bad and if the wind blew the wrong way, the neighbours began to exclaim about the "vile stink around here lately." i recognised it after a day or two and flushed pink each time the breeze whispered her secrets and carried that scent wafting through other people's kitchens, into their babies' sleeping nostrils and all through their dinners and t.v pilates sessions. they didn't get it... wives thought their husbands had forgotten to put out the trash. husbands grew uncomfortable and suspicious. i witnessed.

i knew that i had been driven to commit that act. driven beyond rational. beyond logic and beyond well grounded reason. nothing had made sense in the days leading up to it, i remember that much. he had confused me. i blame him entirely of course.

he was a cool customer (does one say that outside of film noir anymore?) really he was...a dude (does one say that outside of old fonz re-runs anymore?) and i had loved him for a time. his feather tipped hat, a felt trilby worn at a jaunty angle and accentuating his dark eyes and angular bone structure, had caught my eye the first time i ever saw him. the bloody knuckles he put through my door should have alerted me that his hat was simply a distraction, but love blinds people to all but the pretty things don't you think?

i was blinded. i saw only that hat, those eyes, that magnetic charm captured me and i lost my flight in that moment. i felt my wings up and leave the moment i returned his gaze and his smile. when i said hello i swear i heard an angel curse like an unrepentant sinner.

my mother gasped and stepped back (she later pretended she had felt faint and that it was nothing to do with him). my father shook hands and fought the urge to strangle him there and then. he didn't of course, he simply shook hands and said "pleased to meet you" in a tone conveying some kind of masculine message that i did not recognise. they let me walk out of that room with him. the hotel room. they were powerless to have done otherwise and they prayed that my survival skills were greater than his violence. the wind was now telling the neighbourhood that they were.

he had tried to strip me of my sense of right and wrong, reasonable and unreasonable, to the point when my instincts were so dulled that i would have offered up my wrists for him to cut had he told me a bracelet would fit better over the wounds. how do you get back from there? from that place of total annihilation of spirit? "it's either him or you" i heard that cursing angel yell..."him or you." there was no middle ground.

and now the smell threatened to betray me.

cockroach

i needed to get this out...i needed to exorcise my demon and look down upon it, slain. lying dead on my carpet. carpet would've definitely been best; it would have irritated her the most. mess. disorder. lack of control.

when we arrived, there were crumbs scattered all around the bin, clearly she hadn't ever been there; the place would have been immaculate otherwise. devoid of character, polished into oblivion. and so the debris led me to wondering if mice and other rodents were somewhat like ants, in that rather than clear *up* all of the waste, they left little piles of their own chewed up, spat or shat out mulch as evidence of their presence? were there rats and mice in this place, or more likely still, were there cockroaches?

i imagined her licking their purple~black carapace and gained some really sick pleasure from envisioning the look of distaste upon her face...obsessive compulsive licking disorder. go on, lick it, i believe it can make you high you know, they use it in artists glazes and such and you really should try it...lick lick lick as she filled herself with self loathing, confusion and the weak willed accommodation of everything and everyone but her own desires. i would lick this dirty animal for you because i love you so much she would say.

in the morning, the scattered remnants were still there so either the rodents and roaches were elsewhere or the maid was shit or she the one who was supposed to have banished the debris had been resting with a migraine or something. i imagined the chelsea hotel dirt distressing her and the paintings upsetting her. i imagined the room demanding a refund from her...these guests were really not up to standard concierge....do something about them will you, and the room spat them out onto chelsea streets and chill winter winds. i imagined her pan-handling to make a buck or two and maybe selling herself to get a room or food for the night. i imagined her desperate to keep warm and considering whether heroin or the blankets in the night shelter would do the job best. somehow it seemed easier to imagine her whoring herself than fucking her lover.

we emerged from that room and that enormous bed, having fucked at least twice a day, painted, written or read something at least once a day and been affected and changed by it in every moment of the day. we came back and i dreamt of people trying to kill us and you hatching brilliant escape plans, knowing that our lives were in danger. i knew you would take care of me. fight for me. stand up for me. i knew you would not let anyone fuck with me or do me over. i knew that your fists were like iron in defence of those you love. i never felt anyone stand up for me like that before and i don't think she could handle that. she wilted in the fire. she looked at me like a stanger and i her. she had formulas born of repetitive strain. she was injured. i was tired.

i shut the door of that place, of that hotel and i was changed forever. i am an artist, a lover, a mother, a whore. She knows none of that. she sees shapes and has no idea who i am. she has no idea how to speak to me. i leave her licking the shiny carapaces of cockroaches and other insects. they may take some time to become cleaned to her very high standards but at least she will have something to do. a sense of purpose.

dark

he wants to love her? let him try.

he thinks he can love her? she doesn't.

he thinks he can know inside her? well it's dark in there.

he wants an easy ride? leave now.

once there was a girl. innocent, naive, hopeful. sunny disposition, talks too much, must try harder, tends to get easily distracted by her classmates, a pleasant member of the class. sweet.

once there was a young woman. danger attracted her. clubs, dancing, nightlife, gangsters. little ones at first...the odd kiter, the odd pickpocket, the odd shoplifter, the odd "watch the door while i go in and fucking whistle loud if you see anyone". adrenalin. clean the signatures off the cards. you try.

cars. tdawc. taking and driving away without consent. styal. but i love him dad. no. leaving. no, she won't come home. bye. paco rabanne never meant for cheapskates and thieves. smell it now and it's a thieves smell.

"she's fucking mad hanging around with him. he's a psycho."

"no, you just don't understand him, he's sweet really"

older (not much). manchester clubs, manchester gangland. london. pyscho was fucking right but it's too late now. spiral. darker. down. dark heart. locked her in a room once and left her there, naked, vulnerable, visited.

he thinks he can love her? here, let her give you a clue.

she could punch you when you show her love. how fucked up is that? you offer something beautiful and she wants to jump on it until it is shattered. how fucked up is that? you kiss her, she could cry. but mostly you just walk faster than her. running? who is running the furthest the fastest? her she thinks. who is the most scared? she doesn't know. she doesn't even know if she can love any more. you're testing her and it hurts.

she feels dark but don't offer her pity, offer her nothing, it's more likely she'll understand that. don't offer her compassion, she may bite you. don't offer her secrets, she's got too many of her own. don't offer her tenderness, she doesn't trust it. offer her a fight, she knows how to do those. offer her freedom and run beside her, wind on skin, until you drop, bloody and weeping.

you think you can love her? try

you think you know her? she doesn't know herself yet

love pains her

dirty angel's death wish

slipping further and further into her own mind, the black spaces became somehow comforting and familiar once again. she played amongst shadows and chose headless roses for her bouquet; their petals long since fallen, their thorns reassuringly sharp. she felt at home with the winged and serpent tongued creatures here. they demanded nothing, content simply to fly or to lie in wait for their prey. she was never afraid of them. in the early days, they looked upon her scornfully which had disturbed her until she came to realise that they were themselves in their very essence and could never leave this place whilst she could opt in and out whenever she chose. they despised her for it and yet grudgingly recognised in her a kindred spirit. this would always be enough for her.

there was a strange, haunting odour in the city today. she inhaled deeply, finding it somehow compelling. sometimes when at home, she would take the same comfort from the smell of her own soiled underclothes and whilst this was not the same kind of smell, (it had a metallic base and a lingering aroma not unlike the smell left behind after a firework display. sulphurous and dank yet full of warmth and the last traces of the "ooohs" and "aaahs" accompanying such things), it offered the same kind of refuge to her aching soul. this is me...this is me...this is where i belong and who i am.....

one day, as she was visiting the place yet again, one of the creatures began to circle overhead in a manner quite unfamiliar to her. as the beast descended, she could see that he was not an ugly creature at all, although very unusual in his appearance. it could even be said that his nose was exquisitely beautiful and his eyes the most spellbinding she had ever seen. he alighted beside her, folding his black wings rapidly, though somewhat crudely, and stared at her. she began to perspire. it was unheard of for these creatures to leave the certainty of their own.

he gestured forcefully towards the dirt where they were now both sitting, side by side, beginning an urgent dialogue etched into the surface. a line of unintelligible symbols began to form, and as they did, the woman realised that she was reading and more astonishingly understanding them. contained within their form, a story began to take shape. although he was of another breed, another time, another place, he had been waiting for her. she had called to him once in a dream and upon responding, he was bound to her, for he had recognised the faint silver shards of a glimmering hope in her dreamscape. his darkness had shifted irrevocably in seeing this. he was changed by her. he now needed her, as she needed him. an awkward symbiosis, born of truth and knowing no limitations and inevitably, a painful one; such liaisons were treasonous.

a single tear fell from his dark eyes as he looked at her. she leaned toward him and licked it from his coarse fleshed cheek. ingesting him, she let out the most blood-curdling scream, the sound of it puncturing her ear drums and sending her in turn, into a death convulsion. her body could not contain this pain, this love.

she groped frantically for his hand, and finding it, clung desperately to all she had discovered in this brief moment. simultaneously they uttered the same words..."don't ever leave me again" as their mutual pain took them onto a new threshold, into a new place.

"i've always loved you" he said as her tiny body began the process of disintegration. "i always will"

she unfolded his tightly knotted fist and brushed his palm with the most delicate touch of her remaining fingertip;

"you've got my life in the palm of your hand my love"

they were one and the same. they were love.

feral

The feral thing was violet. A strange shade of violet though; sickly, slightly emerald-green even, but only when seen in certain lights. It bit him and it was then that his skin fell off revealing the bones underneath, all covered in red whelts which were itching like fuck. He tried to cover himself before he realised the futility of it, no flesh on the bones and he was still trying to cover his genitals...ha! he saw the funny side and laughed so fucking hard he began to cough blood. The blood began to drip from everything around him.....cutting, cutting, cutting.....slash, slash, slash...drink, drink, drink.

Vrischika is the Sanskrit word for scorpion. This posture is so named because the body resembles a scorpion with its tail arched above its head ready to sting its victim. Although it may not be a simple posture for beginners to perform, the Scorpion is not as difficult as it may at first seem.

The creature stung him. He hadn't seen her tail, curving over her torso and head, like a flash of unexpected lightning. Something not unlike static electricity was running through him now. His body began to levitate. Suspended in mid air, he yelled at her,

"What the fuck was that?" but his voice sounded like it belonged to someone else.

He fell into what must have been a dreamlike alpha-brainwave state. Somewhere in there, the bouncers were becoming hyenas, laughing like vulgar women in a brothel, only louder and dirtier and with more mockery....at his expense? Or were they just enjoying themselves....he couldn't tell but he was fucked now anyway so he just surrendered to falling further in.

The blood was seeping out of every orifice and every gash, slash and cut. The blood...he dressed himself in it and admired his new red suit.

"Sweet" he said, nodding in appreciation.

Well dressed no in his bright red blood suit, the bouncers let him in.

She hadn't needed to sting him really but it had served her purpose in taking him out of her immediate vicinity, and now, he was out of control which he would hate! Puppet Mistress was holding court. She demonstrated by pulling on a virtual thread in front of her face. He twitched, ugly dancing....she laughed a vicious laugh....

"Bitch" he thought (or did he say it?). Fuck... even his thoughts were drifting away now, belonging to her...

Lotus pose: The Sanskrit word vajra means thunderbolt or diamond. Make the thighs tight like adamant and place the legs by the two sides of the anus. This is called the Vajra-asana. It give psychic powers to the Yogi.

He found himself contorted into a strange shape, his feet either side of his anus. Even in this dream state he could smell the stink of his own fear, locking him into inertia.

She approached him and coughed from deep within her guts, hocking up the phlegm and spat it with force into his face. Claudia! It was Claudia...how had she done that?!!

Whispering into his ear now, beyond the hearing of her servants or her cohorts....

"My dear sweet Assassin....will you *ever* learn? You think you can fuck with me? Over and over and over you challenge me, and over and over and over you lose...."

Pouting now, her lips as close to his ear, as close to his neck as he could bear without ejaculating prematurely,

"I'm gonna enjoy this baby….I've been practising these poses. Naturally I wouldn't bother with them myself but I knew they'd come in handy for something. Those yoga teachers can harbour some ba-aa-aad-strong evil energy when it's all supposed to be peace and light you know. Works fucking wonders when you need to tap it for other purposes….ready made toxins just waiting to flood your system sweet thing. And now look at you, ready there with your pretty ass all exposed for me….what shall I do with *that* I wonder? Are you feeling that psychic energy baby…do you know what I have in mind for you yet? Oh, I do hope so…I think you'll recall that we tried this once before in my dungeon didn't we…with my cock-gimp…you liked that didn't you baby…perhaps you're ready for more, sweet thing?"

She yanked his shirt to one side and flicked her lighter over his chest, perilously close to his body hair, before lighting her cigarette.

Fuck with your head

i am curled in a corner of dark smoking venom. you approach me too late for me to uncurl. i SPIT. it lands, violent fluorescent pink on your screen, and tells you what *would* have happened had it hit your eye. i bang bang bang against the plastic screen, looking for release.

you lie drift, drift, drifting into sleep. you sleep with your routines, you eat with them, you find peace in them. as i find peace in mine. what are mine? who am i?

i tap tap tap on my keyboard into the small rain-sodden nights of howling wind and bleak manchester tomorrows. i love this city. you love this city. we hold each other some nights; rivals in love and in life. i adore you. you worship me. i tease you. you torment me. i love you. do you love me?

you fuck fuck fuck me and i respond to your loving baby. i suck suck suck you and you respond to my desire baby. then you sleep in that man way...'night baby...love you....turn over ninety degrees and make like a log. me, i turn over in that girl way and let my mind run away with me...what does *that* mean? is it this? is it that? how does that work? will it still rain flowers and love hearts tomorrow or will i remember i'm back in a rainy city on a monday night? where am i?

i get up. i was asleep on hour ago...almost...missing you...craving you...needing you...talk to me about bridal gowns and work. talk to me about kids and bills. talk to me about art and music. talk....talk...talk.....

bay~beeeeee......i love you

bay~beeeeeee.... i love you too

arms full of paperwork and a head full of dreams, i search for myself. ears full of music and eyes full of sex, you find yourself. i meet you there...often.....do you meet me in my dreams? alpha male seeks alpha female....strong, consistent, creative, sexy, violently happy, astonishingly lovely. hiss hiss hiss.....

trying hard to think before i speak. trying hard to change the fucking record. tired of that worn out groove. knowing that love is so so simple yet so so fucking complex.

Dear Mr --------

it has come to my attention that you appear not to have filed a recent update on your accounts. furthermore, you appear to be clinging on to habitual behaviours as mirrored by my client Ms. --------. Please amend your records to show 'The Truth' asap.

yours gratefully

fuckwityourhead.co.uk

junkie

i was on my knees. just looked up one day and realised i was down in the dirt, crawlin' in the dust, knees bloodied and red, hands torn to ribbons, scratched, a ton of knots in my hair and dark circles under my eyes you could seat half a cinema in without wonderin' if there was too much light to see by. the nurse shouted me back into rememberin' that i'd been found there, in a heap in that dirt, scabs starting to form, an icy night~time chill enterin' my heart. it wouldn't go away if it took hold, i knew that, but i was past caring.

"hey you, junkie! get up off of that floor girl and get in your bed. you think we're payin' for you to sleep down on them tiles when someone else coulda had your bed? no sir! get in there now!"

bone weary, draggin' them bloody knees into that loveless bed, alarm begins to set in. jesus my legs don't like them sheets. can't stay horizontal neither with all that twitchin', she watchin' me all along tho' so i play dead and let her think i'm restin' like she tells me. she goes after a while, bored of watchin' me if she can't find nothin' to slam me for.

back onto the floor, the cold tiles soothin' my face, the hardness the only thing that makes sense when my belly is curling up in knots and my legs dancin' like i got st. vitus dance and my guts think they want to empty again only there ain't nothin' left but bitter green bile and emptiness now. sweat drips off my bony body onto the tiles and makes little puddles of steam, i swear i'm that hot. the tiles losin' their chill now i move sideways and inch or two. gazin' up now i can see the grey steel bed above me. cold white sheets, grey wollen blanket, itchy...like i needed more itchin' fer fucks sake.

"hey bitch! what you doin' down there again? get up now or i'm callin' the round sister and you're in a lock~up fast!" dragging my bloody knees again i hate you...i look at you and as much as you hate the symbol of me, i hate the actual you. i give you your power cos i ain't got any left in me. can't fight those battles with my body all racked up busy with this one....

morning round ~ doctor: "i think you need a dog. something to be responsible for other than yourself."

morning round later ~ sister: "i think you are ridiculous even considering getting a dog when you quite clearly can't take care of yourself."

morning round patient #1 ~ "see him, he just got back from ect again...he'll be gone now for quite some time. little by little he disappears and each time he comes back he brings less of himself back with him ya know..."

morning round patient # 2 ~ "watch out for her there. she start lookin' at ya, ya move fast! she'll have that table on yer head soon as look at ya." good advice...thankfully i see it comin' at tea time round when the largactyl is wearin' thin. she thinks i'm her son and i can see pure hatred levelled at me in the stare of her glinting eyes. i move just before the table lands.

shit! i gotta get this one sorted.

over the month my sweats get less and less and my belly starts to find that their food that stinks like stewed cabbage no matter what's on the menu is strangely appealing. a hunger is returning. legs have stopped dancin' now and even the knees are scabbing over nicely.

someone lets me down off that cross and i stare, blinded by the light.

scarred heart.

walkin' like a child now. there's nothin' to fill the void. i look up and that nurse is there. she looks into my eye and turns on her heel and walks away. we don't say nothin' to each other. it's all been said.

think i saw that monkey that was on my back jump across in her direction though...weird that huh....

and then a year or more passes and i'm on my knees again only this time, there's no blood and my legs aren't dancin'.

another year or more, or was it a decade or two, and i'm standin' tall, heart full of fire, watchin', wonderin'....

and i have a question....it doesn't matter what the answer is, but i'm curious baby....

snake kiss

the milk was curdled, the dog was limping, the kids were howling from their soggy corner in the damp, linoleum covered bathroom and the fluorescent strip was flickering irritatingly over her head. there was a yellow tinge to her skin again and it hadn't come from some poxy tanning salon anywhere nearby. fuck...she was getting sick again.

she flicked through the local newspaper trying to ignore the increasing noise levels coming from the upstairs bathroom. some fucking nutter had managed to lose a snake and up to now, no-one had managed to re-capture it. why the hell people kept those creepy things she had no idea but as her mascara-streaked eyes scanned the article, she noticed that not only were the flats where it had gone missing in her direct vicinity, but that the reporter skilfully skirted around questions about the snake's toxicity. until she came to the bottom of the page and saw the alert. the snake was known to be skittish, aggressive when cornered and highly toxic. suddenly the yellow tinge on her skin, the kids and the dog seemed like a picnic in the park. she fucking hated snakes.

"kids...get out of the bath now!" she yelled up the stairs. they ignored her of course. they were too busy holding each others heads under the dirty lukewarm water.

"kids!...now!!!!!!" she cried. "just do as you're told for once! is it that fucking hard?"

"aaaaahhhhhh...mummy, you said a rude word" started one. she pushed her fringe back out of her face, struggling internally with a cross between pissed off and guilty. she'd never even wanted kids. she wanted to swear whenever she felt like it, to drink whisky for breakfast if she felt like it, get stoned when her man hadn't come home yet again. to lose herself in some dub beat played as loud as her tinny little sound system would go without busting a circuit. she did not want to measure her pain in this reality. she didn't want to restrain herself in case the kids were in danger or the neighbours complained and got her evicted. she didn't want to wait for ever for her man to come in and take whatever pathetic excuse he threw her way because she was too tired to believe in anything different.

she hauled the kids one after the other out of the bath. three of them. still grubby after half an hour sat in the water. "what the hell do you lot do in there?" she asked, not really wanting or expecting an answer. "go and get dressed now" she said, somewhat more softly. she glanced into their room, chaos as usual, checking to see if there were any possible entrances that a skittish snake might find a way in. none. she left them to it.

dressed, they appeared one by one in the shabby living room.

"right kids, i'm taking you to your aunty lil's"

"but you're not dressed mummy" began the youngest.

"i know baby but mummy is tired, lil's expecting you so i'll drop you in my 'jamas. no-one will see baby" and she smiled a limp, weary smile.

half an hour later she was back. she pushed the key into the lock and stepped into her flat. fuck it was a mess here. she'd never liked this place and now, it was about as homely as a cheap whore's hotel room; crayon on the wall and a littering of broken plastic toys perhaps the only giveaway that it wasn't.

she dragged her dull pink slippers across the hall, moving deliberately towards the kitchen where she opened the cupboard to pull out an open pack of cigarettes from the back. reaching down with her other hand she grabbed the half-empty bottle of whisky from the shelf. it was then that she saw it.

the snake's black eyes were a mix of death, fear and hunter which confused her as it launched itself towards her with the speed of an unstoppable road-kill, sinking its fangs into her arm just above the fading tattoo of her husband's name etched into her flesh in better times.

for one split second the woman saw herself as someone else, but what surprised her more than anything was that she appeared to herself as snake-woman. twisting and writhing on the cold tiles now, she began to foam at the mouth as the venom filtered its way through her system. crying out weakly, she began to feel herself fading into nothingness. it felt preferable to her reality. knowing this, she surrendered.

some time later the woman stood up, dazed, no idea where she was. her skin was covered in tiny marks that gave away her transformation. she had lain blind, emptied and poisoned for some time (who knows how long) and waking, had discovered a shed skin on her kitchen floor. licking it tenderly, she had finally managed to let it go, and standing, had gone to look at her reflection. black hunter's eyes, a death of sorts, no trace of fear.

she packed her bag; snakeskin, and left the hovel that had once been hers behind her, realising that the children did not belong to her and the man was a stranger.

devoured

the man stood before her. he stared at her and she wriggled slightly, uncomfortable under his gaze. she'd been there for about three or four days now she thought, though she'd lost track of time in the gradual deprivation of her senses. everything she'd known before had become alien to her in the short time she'd been kept there. her life as it was may as well have belonged to somebody else before the precise moment in time when the man at the bar had caught her eye and her life had changed forever.

she'd willingly gone home with him; sexy, funny and charming, he had easily appealed to her desire for love and companionship above all else. it was when she arrived at his apartment that she began to feel slightly uneasy; just the merest hint at that point but nevertheless evident when she checked in with her gut instinct. it was at *this* moment that she made the (perhaps?) fatal mistake of ignoring instinct in the pursuit of love.

they hadn't fucked. she could say she was somewhat disappointed, but right now the truth was that she was neither disappointed nor relieved because she'd lost her ability to make sense of anything at all. she was disorientated, which was exactly how he wanted her: she was his living experiment.

the young woman squirmed and tugged at her wrist and ankle ties; they were hurting now, and she needed to pee again. she signalled to him, her humiliation just about total with this ritual he had devised in order to meet her basic needs. he arrived with the bedpan, gently lifted her ass to place it beneath her and then watched whilst she peed into it. he removed it with a tenderness that puzzled her, wiped her pussy with a delicate cloth wipe and then left to empty the receptacle.

when he returned, she knew another 'episode' was about to start; she had begun to tap into other secondary senses since being held captive like this. although she'd initially become disorientated very rapidly, she had begun to rely upon her 'sixth' senses much more since that point. she may not have known where she was or why she was there; logic and reason departing, but her sense of hearing had become much, much keener, and her sense of smell was really sharp now, animal almost. sweat, new sweat, a stranger's sweat could make her retch with fear and anticipation. she would know the instant a new person entered the room despite her awkward vantage point; the fear mingling inextricably with the awareness.

she could feel the change in his energy as if it were as real as an electric current passing through her. he was making ready for something; something he in turn feared. a tear dropped from the corner of her eye which he also wiped away with great tenderness, and then smiled softly at her.

five others entered the room. there had only been one or two on the previous occasions, but she somehow knew that this was different. she recognised the faces of a couple of them who had already 'visited' her and it made her feel nauseous to see them there again. what they'd subjected her to already wasn't far enough removed from her memory. she pulled at all of her ties but it just made her ankles and wrists burn and sting on the existing sores so she gave up trying. she knew it was futile in any case but felt she owed it to herself to try.

"is she ready?" asked one of the group?

"yes...she has been well prepared" replied her captor.

the six people in total, the five and her captor, began to collect a number of things from around the edges of the room. she strained her neck to see but found that there wasn't much movement afforded from the head restraint into which she had been bound. her gaze was meant to be strictly 'straight ahead only' in order that she had no choice but to gaze directly into the eyes of the one who would be coming soon. the group started to bathe her with some kind of warm to hot liquid that felt exquisite on her skin, though it had a strange smell, not dissimilar to the smell of oak-moss resin, or cypress or some other woody plant-based oil. it smelled slightly bitter; a bit like burnt almonds...

the man who had captured her came and placed his face so close to her pussy that she could feel his breath on her vulva. he sniffed her and inhaled deeply of her smell. it was arousing her and she flushed pink, not wanting to admit this to either herself or to her captor.

"please...let me go," she whispered.

where had her voice gone? she was more afraid than she realised....

"sorry...no can do baby; he's expecting you now."

"who is? what the fuck is happening here?" but the man just put his fingers to her lips and hushed her. "such foul language for such a pretty young thing...it's hardly fitting my sweet".

he stepped back a little, clearly satisfied with her 'appearance', and beckoned each person forward one by one.

the first shoved a finger into her pussy which made her yelp: it was unexpected. he pulled it out and licked it slowly, nodding to the man beside her…"yes, she's good" he said, and moved away. she was puzzled, angry and afraid at the same time…

next a woman approached holding the flower of a delicate, fuschia-pink orchid in her palm. she showed it to the captive woman and then knelt before her and pushed it gently into her vagina. the captured woman felt exposed…she had no idea what was happening to her but this ritual was clearly an important part of whatever it was. the young woman felt another tear fall down the side of her cheek, wetting her ear. the next three people who approached her all placed something inside her vagina; the first a small berry or seed of some kind, the second a tiny silver chain and the third, one half of a love heart, not unlike the kind you give to your first teenage boyfriend; each of you wears one half until you part. then when you do, you inevitably despise the thing forever.

finally her captor approached with a small pot containing some kind of heavy viscous oil. he smeared it around her vagina, her labia, a little inside the entrance to her hole and a fingertip of it around her asshole. she looked alarmed but he just nodded to her slowly again. she could feel a deep, throbbing heat rising where the oil had touched her skin. then he placed a drop or two on her lips and rubbed it into her mouth, the inside of her cheeks and onto the tip of her tongue. she gagged and tried not to swallow, but lying prone made her swallowing reflex as inevitable as breathing or she would begin to choke very quickly.

the liquid was making her limbs feel heavy and she started to imagine herself flying off into great clouds of billowing azure blue smoke, a crystal sea of fractured light and form. as she was drifting her sensory signals kicked in automatically, something had changed in the room but she didn't know what. she could hear heavy footsteps approaching and there was a hushed reverie in the room.

"she is ready, and is perhaps the most perfect yet my liege."

she looked in front of her and saw him then. a muscular, well built man-beast of unknown origin. she wanted to scream but her voice was somewhere lost in those clouds. nothing worked; there was no co-ordination or synchronicity left in her. only open exposed flesh and being. the only thing they had left her with was her lace panties which were twisted around one ankle, still as pink and delicate as when she had put them on all that time ago…..

he placed himself between her legs and instructed that her binds be loosened. she exhaled with floods of relief…he was going to offer her free-will? however, with a click of his masterful fingers, he summoned the stirrups to be brought out and fixed beside her, just as she felt four pairs of hands take firm hold of her legs and fasten them securely into the metal hospital examination contraptions. "jesus no…please don't hurt me" she whimpered….

he stood proud and tall; cloaked, and in readiness. the girl's tears flowed easily now, wetting the sheet beneath her and filling her with a sense of increased panic as she recognised that her auto-responses spoke volumes to her. the six people stepped forward and removed the heavy velvet cape from the shoulders of the man-beast and he moved one step closer. he looked her in the eye. his eyes flickered emerald green and were full of lascivious power. he needed her now. she wasn't going anywhere. the helpers then removed the cloth that had been covering his loins and the woman screamed again, only this time she heard herself. the beast had a cock that was a living creature in itself. he was host to an independent life-form and it was clearly hungry, teeth snapping and tongue lolling out in greedy anticipation of her cunt, and she knew it.

the thing held his parasitic attachment in his two hands as it began to screech and take a more accessible form. "feed! me! now!" it commanded and the woman tried in vain to appeal to any last remnant of reason in the people surrounding them. then she noticed the expressions on their faces; uniformly lascivious, and she gave up. she was saving them from themselves; her presence there provided them a necessary shield from their own shadows.

the creature was so close now she could feel the tip of its parasite cock-thing touching her clitoris for the briefest of moments.

it was in *that* moment that she realised, and acknowledged, that she wanted it….badly.

it was braying now to get inside her. it needed her innocence but above all it needed her fear, and her fear was gone. in its place was something like lust. reason told her that this creature was so vile and despicable that there was no way on earth she would surrender without a fight but her pussy was begging for the moment when it would enter her, promising to devour her.

she looked them in the eye…first the man-beast and then his cock-appendage. straight, square in the eye, and the thing flickered a moment. hesitated…

for

one
split
second
that's when everything changed…

its' desire for her cunt was so strong now that it couldn't stop, despite the man-beast's best efforts. the man-beast, being a cerebral creature, recognised what had transpired in the previous moment. the cock-beast, being nothing beyond pure animal instinct, did not. its' white stretched lips were dribbling something like a yellow pus of pre-cum arousal fluid as it neared the girl's vaginal opening. it was sniffing like a stuck pig and wriggling like a kitten in the hands of some callous schoolboy experiment. the girl was both repulsed and fascinated by it; she'd never seen anything so vile and yet it was so clearly hungry for her. the creature's hunger was making her incredibly sexually aroused. she whispered, quiet enough that no-one else could hear her…perhaps the words never even emerged; she couldn't be sure what was real any more. "come on baby…enter me now…push *deep*, and *hard*, and make it better than anything i've ever known….take me to the heights of the heavens and the depths of hell in one single moment of entry….take me now!"

the cock-beast sat with its 'head' at her vaginal opening and then let out an ear-splitting howl which shattered the windows spraying rainbows of cut glass into the flesh of those in the room who were watching. the girl screamed and the creature entered her ferociously at exactly that moment. the light in the room shed fractals all around them which were coming from their combined energies as the thing drove itself further and further into her pussy. the force of it made her gasp and she wept rivers of tears now as it pushed mercilessly and relentlessly into her cunt, making its way up her canal, through her womb, through her belly, towards her heart. it was looking for her heart but she was no longer afraid. surrendering to the cock-beast's thrashing movements; her whole body was electric with sex, pleasure and desire. the two of them were merging. the beast was becoming her, and she, it. no boundaries, everything melting…dissolving. who was she?

now it was the man-beast who was weeping and begging as his cock-appendage was clearly being devoured from the inside out. the girl was looking at him; her tears dried, her lips open around her teeth, back bucking against her restraints. she was arching in ecstatic pleasures like nothing he personally had ever imagined let alone witnessed before. then it came…the sound and smell of death; a darkness that fell and a strangeness in the air that took everyone with it; no question of that. the spectators dropped to their knees, they did not know how to act without a guide. the man-beast went limp and the girl broke her bonds as effortlessly as had they never been there. she sat up. her cunt was dripping a globulous mix of blood, semen, the beast's decaying flesh and her own cum…she rubbed her hands into it and then pulled it across her face, her hair, down her chest and torso, and her back. she spread it into her thighs, her calves, her feet, and then wiped it around her mouth and licked her palms clean like a preening cat.

"i think you under-estimated me," she said as she left the snivelling pile of bodies in the room.

"that was possibly the best sex i've ever had…."

and with that, she was gone.

If you enjoyed this book, you might enjoy these titles from our affiliate range, Paraphilia Books:

THE SEVENTH SONG OF MALDOROR

D M Mitchell

A deranged serial-killer goes on a rampage of sexual atrocity across a Europe falling apart in the wake of an unspecified global crisis. But is he what he seems? A cast of implausible characters in a (to say the least) unreliable narrative push the boundaries of credibility and expression. Dreams and nightmares, desire and delirium, all melt together into a metatextual puzzle. A psycho-sexual anti-novel that owes much to its transgressive ancestors – Sade, Lautreamont, Bataille, Artaud with more than a dash of Burroughs and Lovecraft thrown into the cauldron.

Paperback: 186 pages
Language: English
ISBN-10: 1449518125
ISBN-13: 978-1449518127

(www.paraphiliamagazine.com/books.html)

THE MEMBRANOUS LOUNGE

Hank Kirton

Welcome To The Membranous Lounge! Where ugliness and beauty melt and run together, where reality is temperamental and the boundary between "normal" and grotesque is nebulous.

The Membranous Lounge is a zone of slippage, a twilight area between the layers of the world that are familiar and the terrifyingly unknown. It is a chimerical realm inhabited by the hopeless, dispossessed, and those who have simply turned away.

Imagine if Ray Bradbury and Jeri Cain Rossi had a child that they locked away from the world, with only the Marquis De Sade for reading matter, and a dietary intake of bad LSD and atrocious B Movies. The Membranous Lounge would be the spawn of that child's imagination.

With an introduction by **Jim Rose**

Paperback: 140 pages
Language: English
ISBN-10: 1452816301
IABN-13: 9781452816302

(www.paraphiliamagazine.com/books.html)

MESSAGES TO CENTRAL CONTROL

A D Hitchin

A shifting collage of condensed micro-novels; intense and corrosive uzi-bursts of poetic anti-narrative from some alternative cyberporn universe intersecting ours. Reading this book is like surfing the shortwave band and finding oneself listening to alien soundtracks.

"*Messages to Central Control* is a daring and challenging work, and from the outset notions of stable form, content and author are all thrown into question, and the reader is compelled to leave everything they believe in at the door, and to enter with eyes – and mind – open."

From the introduction by **Christopher Nosnibor**

With artwork by **D M Mitchell**

Paperback: 216 pages
Language: English
ISBN-10: 1453865853

(www.paraphiliamagazine.com/books.html)

PARASITE (VOLUME ONE) PARASITE LOST

D M Mitchell

When David Michael K visited The Doctor's office, housed in the mysterious Building, he hadn't anticipated his life tipping into madness where reality melted and stretched and fiction merged with real life.

In a satirical romp that sends up postmodernism, popular culture and satirises satire itself, our hero is chased by homicidal drug-dealing clowns, cartoon characters, pink UFOs and creatures of pure nightmare. Is this a serious book disguised as humour? or a joke at the expense of the intelligentsia? Fun stuff.

With an introduction by **Michael Roth**

Cover by **Pablo Vision**

Paperback: 274 Pages
Language: English
ISBN-10: 1453819304
ISBN-13: 978-1453819302

(www.paraphiliamagazine.com/books.html)

A DREAM OF STONE (and other ghost stories)

Edited by Díre McCain & D M Mitchell

A posthuman ghost anthology from the people who bring you Paraphilia Magazine.

"Their name is legion and they stalk among us. Daily tabloids are replete with pages of phone numbers where, for a fee, we can talk with nameless incubi/succubae.

Alternatively, we can venture into the twilight world of the internet, and converse with 'people' who may or may not exist – the technological equivalent of planchette and Ouija board. Who knows what's really on the other end, fastening onto our insecurities, desires, and fears?"

(from the introduction)

Paperback: Pages
Language: English:
ISBN-10: 1466437944
ISBN-13: 978-1466437944

(www.paraphiliamagazine.com/books.html)

Please check out Paraphilia's free online magazine at:
www.paraphiliamagazine.com